The Ex Games

Part III

J. S. Cooper & Helen Cooper

Table of Contents

Prologue

He watched them as he'd been asked to, snapping photograph after photograph. They looked happy and in love. This was one assignment that made him satisfied. She was a good girl: sweet, innocent, smart, and real. She wasn't a gold digger like all the others, and that made him happy.

His phone rang and he answered it eagerly; he was always excited when one of his sons called.

"Dad, I wanted to know if you want to come to dinner tonight? We're going to try out the new Italian place on Amsterdam."

"Sure, I'll be finished with work in about an hour." He turned the ignition in his car as he watched the couple leave the restaurant. "But I gotta go now. I'll see you later, Matt."

He hung up before his son could answer and put his camera on the seat. He couldn't afford to lose them tonight. Mr. Hastings had been very clear in his instructions. He smiled to himself as he thought about the money he was going to receive for the assignment. He looked down at the passenger seat to make sure that the envelope was still there. He would drop it off before going to dinner. Mr. Hastings would have the information to read in the morning. And then he could make his own decisions about what to do.

Chapter 1
Katie

I stepped back into the corridor with my heart pounding. Why was Matt calling Brandon? He didn't know Brandon. Brandon didn't know him. It just didn't make sense to me. What was going on here? I knew I had two choices: I could go and confront Matt and ask him what was going on, or I could pretend I didn't know anything and try to find out the information another way. I stood in the corridor and thought for a moment. Clearly, Brandon knew Matt and Matt knew Brandon. Which meant that Brandon had been playing me from the beginning of my trip to San Francisco. He had used Matt to gain information on me. I didn't know when he had found out about Matt, but I did know that all his questions about my boyfriend were false. Which meant that he was playing me. He had deliberately tried to hurt me. The man I loved had used me. And I didn't know why.

I walked back to the front door and exited quickly. If Matt had kept it a secret from me, it meant that he didn't want me to know. I knew that asking him what was going on wasn't going to result in any real answers either. I was sure he had a lie prepared and ready to go if I ever asked him too many questions. I bit my lip as I walked down the empty streets. It was starting to make sense—well, a bit of it was. I'd always been surprised that Matt had never really tried to touch me. He'd never made love to me, and even his kisses had seemed lackluster at times. I thought it was because he was worried that he wouldn't be able to control himself if we got too passionate. Now I wondered if he had been holding back for another reason. What if Brandon had recently started tracking me like I had been tracking him? What if he realized I was dating Matt and had offered him a large sum of money to not sleep with me and to keep tabs on me? He was trying to dictate my love life even though he had a fiancée and didn't want to be with me himself, other than sexually. Of course he wanted me sexually. We couldn't keep our hands off each other. But that meant nothing special. What was sex, really, at the end of the day?

I didn't want to go right home. I didn't want to involve Meg and worry her. I knew that she was stressed as it was. I mean, who wanted to go from being a lawyer to a bartender?

I decided to slip into a bar to have a drink and think. It would stop me from pulling my hair out and crying.

"Vodka on the rocks, please." I slid onto a barstool and smiled at the bartender. He was cute, with an 'I just arrived in the big city' look.

"No chaser?" He smiled.

"Do I look like I need a chaser?" I shook my head and ran my hands through my hair.

"Long day?"

"More like a long seven years." I sighed.

"Want to talk about it?" He gave me a slow, wide smile and I shook my head.

"You don't have all night."

"I could have all night, if you wanted me to." He stared back at me and looked me up and down. I realized that he was flirting with me, and a rush of warmness fled to my skin. I smiled back at him—a lazy, not-interested-but-thank-you smile—and he leaned forward and grabbed my hands. "Don't decide yet. The night is still young." He handed me a glass and I sipped at the vodka. It went smoothly down my throat, warming me up from the inside, and I started to feel a little more relaxed.

"Sex is about power for men. Why is that?" I spoke to the bartender, who had stopped in front of me.

"I don't know. Because women let it be about that?" He shrugged. "So you're mad about a guy? Let me guess, you and your long-term boyfriend recently broke up because you caught him cheating?"

I laughed as he stared at me, looking so confident and sure of himself. He had an arrogant yet sincere vibe about him. I stared at his face clinically. On second glance, he was a lot more handsome than I had first realized.

"So am I right?"

"Does it matter?" I handed him my glass. "Another vodka on the rocks, please. Make it a double."

"Drinking away your sorrows?"

6

"More like drinking away the questions in my head."
"Why don't you do what we guys do? Just fuck someone else.
It's the quickest and easiest way to get over someone."
"I wish it was that easy." I stared at the counter. I hadn't had
sex with anyone other than Brandon. I didn't even know what it
would feel like to be with another man. I guess I knew why Matt
hadn't been interested now. Though I wish I knew the full story.
Beep beep.
I picked up my cell phone and saw a text message from
Brandon. I glared at the phone and put it back in my pocket
without reading the message. I didn't care what he wanted. I
grabbed the new glass that the bartender handed me and
downed the vodka in two gulps. I pulled my phone out of my
pocket and read the message. I couldn't resist checking it.
"Call me. Now."
I stared at the message for a few minutes before deleting it and
putting my phone into my pocket. Who did he think he was?
Call him now? Why? Had Maria stepped out to go the gym or
something? I was done with being used and abused by him. I
was not his plaything.
"Another double, please." I smiled at the bartender and played
with my hair.
"Do you want to wait a bit?" He frowned as he looked at me.
"You're too pretty to get drunk and make bad mistakes tonight."
"What if you're the bad mistake?" I flirted with him and he
paused as he stared at me. He shook his head and poured
some more vodka into a new glass.
"Here." He handed me the glass and his fingers grabbed mine.
"But this is the last one. If we go home together, I want to know
it's because you wanted to be with me and not because you're
drunk."
"You're pretty full of yourself." I raised an eyebrow at him,
leaned forward, and slowly licked my lips. "If I want another
drink, I expect another drink."
"And if you want to fuck me tonight, you need to slow down," he
whispered against my lips lightly and his tongue licked my
lower lip slowly. I sat back and looked at him in a daze.
"You kissed me." I stared at him in shock, rubbing my fingers
against my lips.
"That wasn't a kiss." He winked at me.

7

"Your lips touched mine."

"Come here." He leaned toward me and I stared up into his bright green eyes in wonder. He bent down and grabbed the back of my head, and his lips pressed against mine firmly as he kissed me properly this time. I felt his tongue trying to work its way into my mouth, but even though I enjoyed the kiss, I wasn't ready to make it more intimate. I pulled away from him, dazed. "Now that was a kiss." He grinned and walked to the other side of the bar to help another customer.

Beep beep.

My phone vibrated and buzzed again. I grabbed it from my pocket and checked my messages. It was Brandon again.

"Katie, you need to call me now."

"Whatever," I mumbled under my breath. "So you can fuck me and leave again?" I was about to put my phone back in my pocket but decided to text back instead. *"Fuck off."* I pressed send.

Within seconds he had replied. *"I can't without you."* I stared at the words, confused.

"That makes no sense," I texted back quickly, wanting to stop responding, but not knowing how.

He texted back immediately again, and for a second, my heart soared that he was thinking of me. *"Call me, Katie. I want to hear your voice."* I stared at his words and wanted to throw the phone to the ground and stomp on it, and then I wanted to stomp on myself. Why was I so happy at his words? Why did I feel like I was flying just because he had texted me a bunch of crap? I wanted to delete his messages and him from my life. I rubbed my lips again, thinking about what the bartender had said. Maybe I did need to have sex with someone else. Maybe that would be the easiest way to get over Brandon. I didn't want him to have this hold over me anymore.

Beep beep.

The phone vibrated again and I stared at the latest message. *"Are you there? Call me, now."* I stared at the phone, feeling tired. My brain was overwhelmed by everything that had happened in the last couple of weeks. And then the phone started ringing. I answered it without thinking.

"Hello?"

"I told you to call me." Brandon's voice was angry.

8

"So?"

"I want to see you."

"I don't want to see you." I glared into the phone. "What's the *problem*?" I hissed.

"What?"

"Nothing," I mumbled. I didn't want him to know that I knew that he knew Matt. Not yet. Not until I decided what I was going to do.

"I miss you, Katie."

"Where's Maria?"

"Does it matter?"

"What do you think?" My voice rose. "You're an asshole."

"I don't love Maria." His words were firm.

"Piss off!" I shouted into the phone, though my heart leaped with joy at his words. My brain screamed at me to stop feeling excited.

"I want to hold you," he drawled. "I've missed hearing your voice."

"I've got to go," I mumbled, not really wanting to hang up.

"Don't go. Not yet." His voice was urgent. "Where are you? Let me come and take you home."

"How do you know I'm not home?"

"Where are you, Katie?" His voice was harsh.

"What do you care?" I went to have another gulp of vodka, but it was all gone. "Hey, bartender, come here," I called out. He walked over to me slowly with a wicked grin on his face.

"How can I help you, beautiful? Want another kiss?" He laughed and I shook my head.

"Another vodka, please. We can talk about the kiss later." I giggled at him, wanting Brandon to hear the conversation.

"Where the fuck are you, Katie?" Brandon's voice was angrier than I had ever heard before.

"Sorry, I have to go now. Tell Maria I said hello." And then I hung up and turned the phone off so that I wouldn't have to hear it beeping or ringing anymore.

"Who was that?" The bartender handed me a new glass, and I sipped eagerly.

"This tastes like water," I groaned, annoyed and ignoring his question.

9

"That's because it is." He stared at me. "I don't get involved with girls who have issues or relationship problems, but I'm going to make an exception for you. The only thing is, I don't want you to be passed out when we hook up."

"That's assuming a lot."

"You want to get over your ex, right?" He shrugged. "Trust me, when I'm done with you, you won't even remember his name." I sat back, sipped the water, and tried to stop the rush of tears that came to my eyes. I couldn't look at the bartender. It didn't matter how hot he was. I couldn't sleep with him, not when all I wanted was Brandon. The bartender stood in front of me, licking his lips sensually, and I jumped off of the barstool and ran out of the bar, not even remembering to pay. I ran down the street, crying and thinking about what the bartender had said so casually. He'd said that by the time he was finished with me, I wouldn't even remember Brandon's name, and my heart broke. I didn't even want to think of a possibility where I couldn't remember Brandon. I loved him with all my heart. And even though my heart was breaking, I didn't want to move on with some casual sex. Not yet. Not now. Not when every part of me was crying out to be with the man I loved. The man I had spent the last seven years thinking about. I loved him as much as I hated him, and I wanted to make him pay. But I needed to do it on my terms. And I needed to plan it out. That was the only way I could be sure that I could finally move on.

I sat on a bench in Central Park for about two hours before some policemen moved me on. I saw the concern in their eyes as they looked at my tear-streaked face, but they didn't ask me what was wrong. I suppose they knew better than to ask a crying lady what was wrong unless she was walking up to them with an issue. I was tired when I finally got to my apartment complex. I was standing at the main door, searching for my keys when I felt someone grab me. I tried to scream, but my voice was hoarse and nothing came out.

"Where have you been?" Brandon's nostrils flared as he stared down at me with darkened eyes.

"Out." I pulled away from him, my heart beating faster.

"With the bartender." His voice was angry and he held me tight. "Did you fuck him?"

10

"It's none of your business." I glared up at him and tried to push him away.

"Tell me." His voice was hoarse and his eyes looked into mine, searching for an answer. "Did you fuck him?"

"What do you care?"

"Does your boyfriend know you're tramping it around the city?"

"How dare you!" I found a sudden burst of energy and pushed him off of me. "Just leave me alone, jackass."

"Where have you been? I've been waiting for you to come home for the last two hours."

I turned my face away from him, not wanting to answer.

"Your phone isn't on." He pulled me towards him again. "I've been calling and calling. I thought something happened."

"As you can see, I'm fine." I rolled my eyes.

"Act your age, Katie," he hissed, angry again. "You're not eighteen anymore."

"And you're not my boyfriend anymore." I stared at him and laughed bitterly. "You may think you can have me when you want me, but those days are gone. I'm not going to sleep with you again."

"Is that so?" His eyes glittered like diamonds in the dark.

"Yes." My hands crept to his chest to push him away again, but instead they caressed his pecs. "You're never going to have this"—I pointed to myself—"again."

"But what if I want it again?" He tilted his head and stared at my breasts. "What if I want you tonight?"

"I don't think you want sloppy seconds," I shot back at him. He drew his breath in sharply.

"I know you didn't sleep with that man." He pushed me back against the doorway and I gasped.

"How?" I squeaked out with eyes wide open.

"Because," he said as he leaned towards me and pressed his lips against mine, "you're mine." His hand slid up my shirt and cupped my right breast. "Your body is mine. I possess you and only I can have you." His lips crushed down on mine and my legs buckled slightly as my body convulsed with pleasure underneath him.

"I'm not yours." I shook my head as my hands ran up his back. "You have a fiancée," I whispered against his lips. "You have a son."

11

"You're still mine," he growled against my lips. "I told you that night in Doug's, if you continued on that night, if we made love, I would possess you. I'm never going to let you go."

"I'm quitting," I whispered before his tongue entered my mouth. I was too weak to say no. I held on to his shoulders as his tongue explored every inch of my mouth. He pushed himself into me and I felt his erection against my lower belly. His fingers squeezed my nipple and his lips were dominating mine in their quest.

"You're not going anywhere." He leaned back and stared into my still stunned eyes.

"You can't stop me." I shivered as his fingers switched to my other breast. A man walked past us in the street and I could see him staring at us and mumbling something to himself. I was half surprised that he hadn't stopped to watch the show. "I have to go inside now."

"I'm coming up."

"No." I shook my head. "No, you can't."

"I want to see your apartment." He smiled then. "I've never seen any of your apartments."

I stared at him then as I realized that he was correct. "How did you know where I live?" I frowned as it dawned on me that I had never given him my address.

"There's nothing about you that I don't know, Katie." His eyes pierced into mine. "Now let me in, or I'll make love to you in the street."

"You'd like that, wouldn't you?" I glared at him. "Why don't you just bend me over the dumpster again and leave?"

"I made a mistake," he sighed. "I shouldn't have done that."

"Well, you did."

"Are you ever going to forgive me for that?"

"I already forgave you," I said softly, and his eyes looked at me in hope. I felt weird as he stared at me. It almost felt like he still cared, but he'd fooled me once before. "I forgave you for that, but I don't forgive you for fucking me while you have a fiancée."

"Did you enjoy his kiss?"

"What?" I stared at him, confused. "What are you talking about? I'm talking about you having sex with me while you have a fiancée."

12

"Did you enjoy it when the guy in the bar kissed you?" His body looked stiff and his expression was frozen.

"Why are you asking me this?"

"No reason." He shook his head and sighed. "I should go."

"Don't let me stop you."

"Let me see you upstairs to your apartment first."

"No."

"Katie."

"Fine." I sighed, not wanting to be away from him just yet anyway. I opened the front door and we walked up the stairs slowly until we got to the third floor. "Okay, see ya." I stopped outside a door and he laughed.

"I know you live on the fifth floor, Katie. I also know there is an elevator in this building."

"How'd you know that?" I asked grumpily.

"I own the building."

"Oh." I frowned and my mind started churning again. "Since when?"

"Does it matter?"

"I guess not." I shrugged. "Fine, come on." I started up the steps again and then stopped, feeling out of breath and tired.

"I take it you don't walk up the stairs much?" He grinned.

"I'm just tired," I said, panting.

"You need to work out more." He laughed at me as I bent over, trying to catch my breath.

"Are you calling me fat?" I asked him indignantly.

"No." He grabbed me and picked me up.

"What are you doing?" I struggled against him.

"I'm carrying you up, of course." He walked up the stairs easily with me in his arms. When we got to the fifth floor, he walked directly to my apartment and then put me down. "Open the door," he ordered me.

"Yes, sir," I muttered back to him.

"I like it when you call me sir." He grinned.

"Don't get used to it," I shot back.

"Trust me, I know." He followed me into the apartment. "You like to be on top too much to be a submissive."

"Shut up!" I gasped and hit him in the arm. "You can leave now."

"I don't want to leave." He shook his head.

13

"Shh." I made a big deal of telling him to be quiet. "Meg is probably sleeping. I don't want to wake her."

"Then let's go to your room."

"Sorry, but I have someone coming over." I stared at him. "He won't appreciate you being here with me."

"Who's coming over? Matt?"

"No, the guy in the bar. He was a bartender. He's coming here after work. So I need to go shower and get ready for him now."

"Are you trying to bait me, Katie?" His voice was low as he took a step toward me.

"No." I shook my head and took a step back.

"What's his name?"

"Whose name?" I blinked at him, trying to think fast.

"The bartender."

"I didn't ask him his name." I swallowed hard. "We kissed and then fucked and then I left to get the apartment ready."

"You didn't fuck him." Brandon shook his head, looking furious.

"Maybe not, but I thought about it." I stared at him straight on. "As he kissed me, I thought about fucking him hard. I almost came just thinking about it."

"I'll make you pay for that." His voice was low as he grabbed my arms and pulled me toward him.

"What are you doing?" My breathing was hard and my body was trembling in sweet anticipation.

"I'm going to make you wish you had never met that bartender."

"He tasted like cotton candy and gin," I whispered against his lips. His eyes darkened as he gaze turned murderous. His lips crashed down on mine hard, his teeth biting my lower lip aggressively as his tongue plunged into my mouth. His kiss was all-consuming and devastating. This wasn't a sweet kiss of love; this was a kiss of passion and domination. I melted into his arms as he made me his once again. My every nerve ending responded to his colonization, and I whimpered when he pulled away from me slowly, running his hands through his hair as he stared at my lips.

"You're bleeding."

"It doesn't hurt." I licked my lips and tasted a faint drop of blood.

"It's nothing." He bent down again, and this time his tongue licked my lips softly before he sucked on my lower lip. "What are you doing?"

14

"Licking the blood away."
"Are you a vampire?" I joked and he laughed as he pulled me toward him and kissed my forehead.
"When I'm with you, I feel like I could be one."
"What does that mean?"
"Nothing." He shook his head. "Let me see your room."
"No."
"That's not go through this again." He grabbed my hand. "Take me to your room."
"I can't."
"Stop with the games. We both know no one is coming tonight. I'm already mad enough that you kissed someone else."
"Whatever." I tried to pull away from him as my insides grew warm with desire.
"Katie." He pulled me toward him again and looked down at me seriously. "Don't push me."
I wanted to whisper, "Or what?" but no words would come out. He squeezed my hand and led me to my bedroom door. I frowned as he walked in and locked it behind us. He pushed me down on the bed and then lay down next to me. His hand ran up my stomach and to my breast, and he gazed at me with lust in his eyes.
"I'm going to make sweet love to you, Katie. Like you want me to."
I stared at him, unable to deny that I wanted him.
"Don't kiss anyone else." His voice sounded strangely bleak.
"I can kiss who I want." My heart started pounding.
"I'll leave Maria." His words were soft, but they grinded my heart to a stop.
"What?"
"I'll break the engagement off with Maria." He held my hands.
"If that will stop you from being with other men."
"What about Harry?"
"Let me worry about him." He averted his gaze from mine.
"I don't understand." I looked back at him. "Do you still love me?" I was hopeful as I stared at him in front of me, all broody and dark. I felt like I was at the edge of a cliff about to jump into the water and only he could stop me from jumping.

"I never stopped loving you, Katie." The words made my heart jump, but his expression was still dark and tormented. "It's never been about me loving you."

"Then what's it been about?" All color left my face as I stared at him.

"It's been about you and if you're ready. If you've finally grown up. If you see love as a real and deep emotion that can't be toyed with or if this all still a game to you." His words sounded angry.

"I see." I swallowed hard, upset inside. His words had hurt me. I couldn't believe that once again he was harping on about my age. Was I never going to be able to move on from that one small lie?

"Your skin is so soft. It reminds me of rose petals." His fingers trailed down my cheek and his lips nibbled on my ear.

"Why are you changing the subject again?" I breathed out, running my hands through his hair.

"What do you want to talk about?" he whispered in my ear.

"Are we getting back together?" I whispered back, turning my lips to his.

"Let's talk about this later." His lips came down on mine and I closed my eyes as I melted into him. My brain was happy and my heart was dancing. Brandon was going to leave Maria, and that was all I cared about. Maybe we really did have a shot at a future together. And then I felt my insides freeze. There was still the issue with Matt. How did he know Matt? How could I be sure he wasn't playing me again?

"Let me be on top." I pushed him down on the bed, slowly unbuckled his belt, and pulled his pants down. His cock struggled against his white boxer briefs and I groaned as he pulled me down on top of him.

"See how hard I am for you?" he growled against my ear as he pulled my top off. He unclasped my bra and threw it on the floor before pushing me up slightly and taking my left breast in his mouth. My body shuddered as his hands slid down my back and squeezed my ass. His fingers quickly undid my pants and I wiggled on top of him as he pulled them down my legs. I pulled his boxer briefs off slowly as I kissed down his stomach, and I smiled to myself when his body stilled as my mouth neared his hardness. I kissed down his shaft softly, enjoying the feeling of power I had over him in this moment. I could make him cry out my name and beg me to satisfy him if I wanted to. I took him into my mouth and he groaned as I sucked on him wholly. I loved the salty, raw taste of him. He was all man and I was all woman, and I held his fate in my mouth. I took him deep into my mouth, wanting to taste every inch of him. His cock jittered in my mouth and he looked up at me with a hooded gaze. "Katie," he groaned as I slowly pulled back and sucked on his tip, licking the pre-cum off of the tip before sitting up and sliding my body onto him. I positioned the head of his cock between my legs and allowed the tip to gently rub my clit as I moved back and forth, pleasuring myself with him. "Katie," he groaned louder this time. "Please."

I smiled down at him, almost forgetting that I hated him as much as I loved him. All I could think of was Matt's call. What problem did they have? I needed to know how Brandon knew Matt. I reached down and caressed his cock again before slowly sliding down on it. I moaned as he filled me up and my juices covered his hardness. I sat on top of him and rode him slowly, allowing his cock to slide in and out of me before twirling my hips. He groaned as I increased my pace, and I watched as he closed his eyes. I looked down at him as I fucked him, and I knew that this was my opportunity to get some answers. I increased my pace even more, and his hands reached up to grab my breasts as I rode him. And then I slowed my pace until I completely stopped moving.

He opened his eyes slowly and groaned. "Don't stop, Katie."

"I want to ask you a question," I said softly and moved back and forth slowly. I could feel his cock twitching inside of me.

"What?" he groaned as his hands moved to my hips to try and force my movements to go faster.

"I want to know how you know my ex-boyfriend, Matt?" I sat up until his cock was completely out of me and then sat back down and started grinding on him but not allowing him to enter me.

"Katie." His eyes darkened as he tried to adjust his cock to be inside of me.

"Tell me." I reached down, grabbed his cock, and let the tip of him enter me. "How do you know Matt?" I thought I had won as he groaned and sat up slightly, but then Brandon grabbed ahold of me until I was flat on my stomach. I felt him lower his body onto mine before slipping his cock back inside of me. He moved quickly, and I closed my eyes as pleasure overtook everything in my mind. I gasped as I felt him going deeper and deeper. He then pulled out quickly and flipped me onto my back before entering me again.

"I want to see your face when you come for me." He grinned down at me as he increased his pace.

"Tell me," I gasped. "How do you know Matt?"

Brandon was quiet for a moment as he fucked me. I could feel his orgasm building up, and my body started shuddering as his fingers played with me as he fucked me. I closed my eyes as my orgasm built up, and he slammed into me a few more times before I felt him burst inside of me. I climaxed a few seconds after him and clung to him as our bodies shook together.

"His dad works for me," he whispered in my ear. "Matt is Maria's brother."

Chapter 2
Brandon

Matt's phone call had stopped my heart. I hadn't waited all these years and come this far for Katie to just give up on me. I couldn't let it happen. I wasn't going to let it happen. All my life I had gone from woman to woman, not knowing what love was and not caring, and then I met Katie. Katie of my heart and soul. Katie who set my heart on fire with one smile. The moment I saw her, I knew she was the one. Something about the way her eyes stared into mine with her shy smile, the way her hair always curled no matter how much she straightened it. There was something about her that couldn't be tamed. Yet, she appealed to me. She was the love of my life. But now, she was giving up on me.

I watched as Harry played with his Legos, carefully pushing the pieces on top of each other. I loved him more than life itself. My son, the flesh of my loins. I'd never experienced a love like this before. He was the symbol of all my dreams come true, and I would not let him experience the pain I'd had to experience. Before I made any changes in our lives, I had to be one hundred percent sure that he wasn't going to get hurt. That was why I'd left Katie early this morning. I knew she would be upset that I had left while she was asleep, but as I'd lain with her, watching her sleep, I'd known that I was too weak. I hadn't wanted to leave. I hadn't wanted to let her go again. It was becoming increasingly hard to not say to hell with everything and just stay with her. But there was too much at stake. There was Harry to think of now. And I knew that, to a lesser extent, I had to take Maria into account. And my promise to Will. And I couldn't forget what had happened with Denise. I closed my eyes as I thought about Denise—she was the reason for all of this. If I could only turn back time—then I wouldn't be in this mess.

Last night had been hard. When Matt called me, I knew that I didn't have much time left. I couldn't let her leave Marathon Corporation. I knew that if she left, everything would have been for naught. I was mad at myself when I got off the phone with Matt. I had pushed Katie too far and too fast, and she was already breaking. And now she had kissed another man. I wanted to hit someone at the thought. I grew angry and jealous at the thought of her making love to another man. She hadn't last night, but who knows what stopped her. I was sure that it hadn't been for the lack of the bartender trying. I was going to have to find out what bar she had gone to and have a *talk* with the bartender, just in case Katie went in there again and had any ideas. My insides felt like they were going to burst out of my stomach. I clenched my fists as I thought about her kissing another man and enjoying it. I had done everything in my power to get us to this moment, and it wasn't working out as planned. Not at all.

I thought back to the first night I met her. It was the best and worst night of my life.

The first time I saw her was at 1:30 a.m. I could still remember it as clear as day. I had been walking home when I saw her standing there, looking so lost and innocent. She had been standing against the wall and dancing and singing to herself with a huge smile on her face. I hadn't been able to stop myself from going up to her, even though I hadn't wanted to. My insides had screamed at me to move on, but there was something about her that had made me grind to a halt.

"Are you okay?" Outside the trashy club, I'd approached her apprehensively, hoping not to scare her.

As I got closer to her, I realized that her face looked pale. I immediately felt concerned for her, though my brain was screaming at me to leave her alone. I knew that Doug's was a bar full of miscreants, and after the last couple of weeks I'd had, I wasn't interested in meeting any new women.

"Do you need me to take you somewhere?" The words were out of my mouth before I could stop them, and my hands gripped her shoulders. As soon as I touched her, I felt a buzz of electricity run through me. She looked up at me then, her big brown eyes friendly and surprised. She studied my face for a few seconds before grinning at me in appreciation.

"I'm fine." She giggled slightly and moved closer to me. A part of me wanted to kiss her right then and there. She captivated me with her openness. It was something I wasn't used to. "I'm just waiting on my friends." Her words slurred and she hiccupped.

I looked around the street to see if I could see any other girls. There was no one else outside, aside from one of the bouncers and a seedy looking man who was staring at her legs. I glared at him before turning back to her angrily. What was she doing standing outside this sleazy club by herself? Didn't she know what could happen?

"You're drunk. I'm not seeing any friends here."

"They're in the ladies' room." She stumbled towards me.

"I see. I'll wait with you then." I took her hand and we leaned against the wall, waiting for her friends to come out. She stared at me again with a sweet smile.

"Thank you," she said softly and I nodded at her, not knowing what to say.

This girl was different, with her big, wavy hair and cheap, overdone makeup. She didn't fit the sleek, made-up look of other women in the city. A part of me was attracted to her for all she represented, and the other part of me was attracted to her because she was sexy as hell.

"Are you trying to seduce me?" She wiggled her eyebrows at me while staring at me with obvious lust as she giggled and pushed her chest out. I appreciated the fact that she was showing me who she was and what she wanted, even though I knew there was no way I would sleep with her now. Not when she was drunk. Not after what had happened with Denise. I'd be a fool to go down that road. I declined her offer and smiled at her. There was something so lost but genuine about her. Standing there brought out feelings I had never felt before. This girl was different, and I was loath to just leave her alone.

I can still remember my brain screaming at me as I offered to take her home with me that night. I suppose I could have asked to see her driver's license and sent her off in a cab, but I wanted to make sure she was okay. And I wanted a chance to see what she was like when she wasn't drunk. I helped her back to my apartment slowly. I was mad at the fact that she went with me so easily. She fell asleep and became dead weight in my arms about two blocks from my apartment, so I picked her up and carried her back quickly, feeling like her knight in shining armor. Only, she didn't know, and I knew that

21

there was no one else who would ever call me a Prince Charming. I'd placed her in the bed and gone to sleep on the couch in the living room. I didn't want her to wake up in bed with a strange man and panic, even though I'd wanted to feel her in my arms.

The next morning she woke up with a trusting face and a huge but weary smile, and I knew she wasn't like all the others. She was different, and as she looked at me so guilelessly, I knew that I wanted a relationship with her. But I couldn't forget what had just happened with Denise, so I called Will and asked him to check her out and follow her. I just needed to know that she wasn't setting me up. It was the second-worst decision of my life, and once again, now I felt like everything was crashing down around me.

"Ow," Harry whimpered, and I was immediately brought back to the present.

"What's wrong?" I hurried over to him.

"My Lego hurt me." He grinned at me and jumped up. "I want to go and play on my new skateboard now."

"Not right now, Harry." I shook my head and ruffled his hair.

"Oh come on, Dad. I'll be careful." He looked up at me with a hopeful expression and a small pout. He reminded me so much of his mother with his expressive face. I hugged him to me for a second and shook my head.

"Maybe tomorrow."

"You always say that." He frowned and pulled away from me. "I'm going to go and play Wii."

"Maybe I'll join you in a few minutes," I called after him as he ran out of the room, and he looked back at me with such a look of joy that I told myself I definitely needed to play with him after my call.

"Hello?" Matt answered slowly and unsurely. I knew he was worried about my tone. I had been furious with him last night.

"Matt, it's Brandon."

"She's not answering my calls, sir."

"That's fine." I bit my lower lip, not sure how to continue. "Right now I need you to focus on something else."

"Sure. Do you want me to look into another company?" His voice grew excited at the possibility, and I sighed internally. He wasn't as good a detective as his father Will had been. I knew his heart wasn't in the job, not if it wasn't to do with business. Matt was a journalist first and foremost, a detective second. And I didn't trust him, not like I had trusted his dad. But when his dad died of a heart attack two years ago, he had taken over the business, and I'd remained loyal to honor his dad.

"No, I need you to find a bar."

"A bar?" His tone sounded surprised.

"I need to know the name of the bar Katie went to last night when she left your apartment. And I need to know the names of all the bartenders that were working last night."

"How am I supposed to find that out?" Matt sounded bored, and I wanted to reach through the phone and smack him. Matt irritated me, and if it weren't for all he'd done so far and all the information he knew, I would have told him what I thought of him. The only reason I'd hired Matt to date Katie was because I knew he was gay. No matter what happened, he was never going to seduce her and have sex with her. And I didn't care about a few sloppy kisses—not from him. I knew he could never set her on fire like I did.

"Do some work." My tone was angry. "Go through her credit card bills, see who saw her in the street, check every neighborhood bar around you with photos, do whatever it takes. But get me that information."

"Sure," he sighed.

"I want it by tonight."

"But I was planning on—" He started and I coldly interrupted him.

"I don't care what your plans were. I need this information by tonight."

"You only care about yourself," he muttered with a bitter tone.

"Don't forget who got you the job at the *Wall Street Journal*," I hissed. "And don't forget who's looking after your sister."

"How is Maria, by the way?" His voice was glib. "Should I reserve a date on my calendar for the wedding?"

"Funny." My tone was anything but humorous.

"I dare say she wouldn't mind being a part of some sort of sister wives marriage," he joked. "Seeing as you like the group stuff anyways."

My blood boiled over at his comment. I knew that he was sending me a warning, not just idly joking. But he had no idea who he was messing with.

"Matt, just get me the information." I hung up the phone and rubbed my temples. That was the problem with having too many people in your business. Will had been the only other person who knew what had gone down with Denise and me that night. And now it seemed that Matt knew as well. I knew then and there that it was over for him as well as for Maria. I'd done as much as I could to help them and honor their father's wishes, but I could take them no further. I didn't care how cruel I had to be.

I called Katie's number and waited with bated breath to see if she was going to answer.

"Hello?" Her voice was standoffish, but she answered after one ring.

"Sorry I had to leave early this morning."

"You did?" Her voice faked surprise. "I didn't even notice you weren't here when I woke up."

"I didn't want to leave." I wished my words could convey the depth of my feelings for her.

"Whatever. You hit it and quit it. That's your usual M.O." Her voice sounded harsh.

"Katie." I was getting angry. "That's not what happened."

"What do you want, Brandon?" she sighed.

"To talk," I said softly, though I really wanted to say, "You. I want you."

"Well, talk then." She sounded irritated. "I have to go."

"Don't quit."

"Maybe you shouldn't have hired your fiancée's brother to date me." She was angry. "And what exactly does his dad do for you?"

"I don't want to talk about it. I told you. Not now." I gripped the phone. I hadn't been completely honest with Katie when she had asked how I knew Matt. I'd been in shock when she asked me, on the point of orgasm, and my brain wasn't able to comprehend the depth of how scared I had been. If she'd stayed around to hear more of Matt's conversation with me, she would have figured out that he was now working for me instead of his dad. There was silence on the phone and my

24

heart dropped. "Katie." I talked into the phone, but I knew she had hung up on me.

I called her back, but this time she didn't answer. I wanted to throw the phone into the wall when I heard the call go to voicemail. I was so angry and worried. What if I had lost her? After everything that had happened, I knew there was a high possibility that she was done with me. And what did I expect? I was forty-two, and she was twenty-five. I'd always wanted to give her space so she could make her own decisions. I'd always known it was a risk and that things might not work out as I hoped. But it had been seven years. I'd sacrificed everything for this moment and opportunity, and it looked like my worst fears were coming true.

"Dad, you coming?" Harry shouted from the living room, and I put my phone in my pocket. I'd try calling Katie again later. Now I needed to be with my son.

***

"I was thinking we should set a date." Maria walked into my study with a tight smile. She had asked me to talk while Harry and I were playing Mario Kart, and I'd told her to come and see me later. Now I wished that I hadn't.

"A date?" I looked up at her blankly.

"For the wedding." She walked behind the desk and sat on my lap. "Silly."

"What are you talking about?" I sat back, uncomfortable with the way she was moving against me.

"I'm ready to get married and make this real." She leaned in toward me and I jumped up.

"This isn't real, Maria." I shook my head as I felt my heart pounding.

"It wasn't at first, but now it is." She stood up and grabbed my shirt. "I know at first you only started dating me as a favor to my dad, but we're in love now."

"Maria, we never dated." I tried to keep my voice gentle, as I knew how fragile she was. "And we aren't in love."

"I love you, Brandon." Her eyes looked upset. "We're a family."

"We're not a family, Maria." I shook my head, fear forming in my stomach.

25

"I spoke to Matt last night." Her voice changed. "I know that Katie's done with you. She's quitting and wants nothing to do with you. It's time to move on now, Brandon," she pleaded with me and her fingers ran down my arm. "It's time to give that dream up."

"That's none of your business, Maria." My voice was hard.

"I'll tell her the truth if you don't marry me." Maria looked up at me with ice in her blue eyes. "I will tell her the truth and that would ruin everything."

"You don't know what you're talking about." I called her bluff.

"My dad told me everything that he did for you." Her fingers ran down the front of my pants, but my cock remained frozen and still. "I know everything." She tilted her head and looked up at me. "What time of year would you like the wedding to take place?"

"Your father would be ashamed of you if he knew what you were doing." I grabbed ahold of her wrist and pulled her hand away from me. "You're disgracing the family name."

"What do I care?" She looked at me with anger in her eyes. "They didn't care about me when they pawned me off to you."

"I've tried to help you."

"Because you love me." Her voice softened and her eyes looked at me adoringly. "You've taken me in because you love me." She rested her head against my chest and I stood there, immobile. I hadn't counted on Maria trying to make this difficult. I decided to save my breakup talk for the next day; I couldn't afford for Maria to go rogue on me—not now. Not when everything was still so precarious with Katie. If Maria really knew everything, then I was in big trouble. She would have the power to topple my deck of cards and have everything come crumbling down around me.

"I have to go out." I extricated myself from her embrace and quickly left the study. Maria was going to make this difficult— very difficult indeed.

"Wait." She grabbed my arm. "Kiss me before you go."

"Maria," My voice was stern as I pulled away from her. "Go and get your bags packed."

"Why?"

"I think it's time for you to move." I cleared my throat. "It's been nice having you here, but it is time for you to move on."

"You told my father you would look after me."

"I've given you a roof over your head. I've protected you as best as I can, but enough is enough."

"It's because of that whore, isn't it? Maria spat out with hatred in her eyes.

"It's time for you to go." I turned around and walked out of the room before I did or said something I would regret.

"You'll never have her, you know!" Maria called out. "Not by the time I'm done. You two will never have a relationship. Not when she knows the truth."

"Maria, I'm warning you." I took a step away from her, hatred burning in me.

"I know about the whores, you know." Her eyes danced with evil joy as she studied me. "And I know about the files. I wonder if innocent little Katie knows. There's quite a lot she doesn't know, isn't there?" She grabbed my hand and placed it on her breast. "Just make love to me, Brandon. Just make love to me so we can make a brother or sister for Harry. Then I won't tell. I won't tell Katie."

"Don't threaten me." My voice was cold and deadly as I pulled my hand away. "You do not want to mess with me, Maria."

"I think it's you that shouldn't mess with me, dear Brandon." She smiled and took a step back. "Where's Harry? I want to go and read him a story."

"He's gone to my dad's house." I felt myself thanking God for getting my dad and his new girlfriend to pick up Harry for the rest of the week. I'd had a feeling that shit was going to hit the fan, and I knew Maria would try to involve him.

"You didn't ask me." She glared at me.

"I didn't need to ask you."

"He's my son!" she screamed, her eyes blazing.

"No, Maria." I shook my head and looked into her eyes. "He's never been your son."

"She's never going to take you back, you know." Her eyes looked at me with a bitter glee. "Not once she knows everything."

I turned away from her abruptly and left the house. I didn't hit women, but I had come mighty close to slapping her. But I wasn't even mad at Maria; I was mad at myself.

27

About thirty minutes later, I found myself outside of Katie's apartment. I needed to see her. I needed to feel her. I called her phone and waited for her to answer.

"Hello?"

"You answered."

"What do you want, Brandon?"

"Can I see you?"

"No."

"Can I come over?"

"No." Her voice was firm. "I'm having an early night. I'm going to bed now."

"I can be there within five minutes."

"Sorry. No." And then she hung up on me again.

I stood there outside her front door, wanting to just open it up and go inside. No one told me no. But I didn't. I knew I couldn't invade her privacy like that. What if she moved out? I couldn't risk losing every connection I had with her. I started walking down the stairs when the phone rang. I grabbed it eagerly, thinking it was Katie.

"You changed your mind?"

"Mr. Hastings?" Matt's voice sounded surprised.

"What is it, Matt?"

"I found the bar." He sounded proud of himself.

"I see. How do you know?"

"There are only three bars near me." His voice sounded obnoxious.

"That doesn't answer my question." My voice grew angry as I became frustrated. "How do you know which one she went to?"

"Well, I happened to be in there just now." His voice was quick and excited. "I was sitting in a corner booth. It's dark in the corners so people can't really see you, but you can see them."

"Get on with it," I growled.

"Well, I was sitting there, and Katie just walked in." My heart stopped at his words and I hit the wall as I exited the building. "And?"

"And the bartender looked up at her and smiled." Matt's voice rose. "And he said, 'Well, this must be my lucky week! I get to see your pretty face two days in a row.'"

"I see."

"So obviously, she must have been there last night," Matt continued. "And I think something happened. Because when she sat down, he offered everyone at the bar blowjob shots. He said that everyone deserved to get as lucky as he was going to get tonight."

"What's the name of the bar?" I growled, furious.

"Getting Lucky," Matt drawled. "I just left the bar and Katie was there flirting with the bartender. He also owns the place. But yeah, the name is Getting Lucky. And I guess we both know what's going to go down tonight."

I hung up, and this time I did throw my phone against the wall. I watched as it cracked and fell to the ground. Katie had blown me off and lied to me. I wasn't happy, and there was no way in hell I was going to let some chump come in and steal my woman away from me. Not after everything I'd been through. Even if I had to play rough and dirty, I was going to make sure that there wasn't ever going to be a relationship between Katie and the bartender.

Chapter 3
Katie

"I don't know if I should take the job." Meg made a face. "Not that I've gotten the job yet. I guess the first interview was just a screening interview."

"A job's a job, right?" I yawned from the couch, my mind elsewhere.

"I'm just not sure if everything is as it seems, you know?"

"What do you mean?" I frowned and looked up at her.

"I don't really know if it's a regular bar. The girl who interviewed me said it was a private club."

"A private club?"

"Yeah, I don't know more," Meg sighed. "I guess I'll find out next week." She sat next to me. "So what about you? Where've you been?"

"Just had to go out for a bit." I leaned back into the couch.

"Brandon was here last night."

"I kinda heard." Meg laughed.

"Oh." I blushed. "Sorry."

"Are you guys back together again?"

"No." I shook my head. "I can't deal with him anymore. I know I've said this many times before, but this time I'm really done."

"It's just all so weird." Meg's eyes grew round. "You get a job at his company and begin a whirlwind sexual adventure with him so quickly."

"Oh, Meg," I giggled. "I don't know that I would say we began any sort of sexual adventure. We had some hot sex a few times and I felt like a fool."

"You're not a fool." She shook her head.

"I'm a fool in love." My phone beeped, but I ignored it and turned to her. "There's something you don't know."

"What?"

"When Brandon bought Marathon Corporation, I wasn't in as much shock as you thought."

"What?"

"I kind of knew he was going to buy the company."

"What? How?" Her voice rose.

30

"Don't judge me," I groaned and leaned back. "This is going to sound crazy."

"Oh my God, Katie. Tell me."

"So you know how much I loved Brandon, right? How much I thought he was the one."

"Yeah." She nodded.

"Well, I guess I never really got over him. I never forgot about him."

"He was a douche, Katie. For what he did. And for leaving you like that. All the things you had to go through by yourself." Meg's voice was passionate. "I'm sorry, but I kinda hate him."

"He didn't know about everything." I bit my lip as I stared at her.

"What do you mean?" She blinked rapidly.

"I mean, I never spoke to him after that day at school. The day he found out I was eighteen. I was hoping he would contact me, but he never did," I sighed. "So I just did what I had to do."

"Oh my God, Katie." Meg's hand flew to her mouth. "But you told me you told him. You told me that he didn't care and he wanted nothing to do with you because you lied."

"I'm so ashamed of myself, Meg." I stared at the wall to avoid seeing the shock in her eyes. "I never told him. I figured if he loved me he would have contacted me. He would have begged me to come back to him. And so I was young and selfish and immature, and I made a rash decision."

"Oh, Katie. Does he know?"

"How could I tell him, Meg?" I shook my head. "There hasn't really been a chance."

"Oh." Meg grabbed my hands and squeezed. "Don't beat yourself up. We all make mistakes."

"Yeah." I gave her a small smile. "So a few years ago, I started really looking into what he was doing. Reading every article I could find about him. Tracking his business stuff, and I even called his office a few times to hear his voice."

"Wow."

"I know, I know. It was crazy. At one point, I almost thought he knew it was me." I sighed. "But I think it was just wishful thinking. I started following a journalist who had written a lot of pieces on him and went to a party that his newspaper was hosting. I knew his photo from the paper, and when I saw him, I accidentally bumped into him."

31

"Oh shit, not Matt?" Meg was bug-eyed now.

"Yeah, Matt."

"I knew you didn't like him!" Meg exclaimed.

"What?"

"He just never really looked like your type. I mean, he was nice and all, but he wasn't really exciting, and you guys never really seemed to have chemistry."

"Yeah, well, get this. So I became friendly with him to try and get more information on Brandon, but..."

"Oh my God, but what?" Meg looked at me with excitement on her face. I knew that she was loving every minute of this scandalous conversation.

"Matt"—I paused dramatically—"is working for Brandon."

"WHAT?" Meg screamed as she stared at me in shock. "Brandon Hastings? Are you telling me that Matt, your boyfriend, works for Brandon, your ex?"

"Yup." I nodded. "Crazy, right?"

"What the fuck?" Meg shook her head. "So was Matt working for Brandon when you met him or more recently?"

"No idea." I bit my lower lip. "That's what I want to know as well."

"This is crazy. You played someone, but maybe you were played from the beginning?"

"Yeah," I sighed. "It's so confusing."

"This is like a frigging movie." Meg jumped up. "I need a glass of wine. Want one?"

"Yeah, go on." I sat back in the couch and waited for Meg to come back with the wine.

"Here you go." She handed me a glass and sat back down. "Okay, okay, so let me get this straight. You tried to find Brandon 'cause you still missed him? Why didn't you just go straight to one of his offices or something?"

"I wanted it to be an organic meeting." I rolled my eyes. "Don't ask. At the time, I thought it was a good idea to make it seem like a chance meeting."

"So you bumped into Matt so you could get insider information on Brandon. Which you got. You then got a job at a company you knew he was buying so that you could pretend to be worried when he was back in your life, but really you were excited. You hooked up with him, hoping that meant that he wanted you back, but instead he treated you like shit again and you found out he had a fiancée and a son. Then you slept with him again and he treated you like shit again. And now you want to leave the job and forget any of this ever happened."

"I guess that's why you're the lawyer." I gave her a half smile. "You got it all in one paragraph."

"Well, I'm no longer employed as a lawyer." She made a face. "But this is one hell of a story."

"I know. I feel like a bit of a psycho," I muttered, thinking about everything. "I can't believe I've wasted so much time on this guy and he's just an asshole."

"I agree that he's an asshole, but I think he deserves to know the truth," Meg said softly, and I looked up into her earnest eyes with a frown. "I know it's hard, Katie. And you probably try not to think about it, but I think you need to tell him what happened. Maybe that's part of the reason why you can't move on."

"It hurts too much." I bit my lower lip, desperately trying to forget what I'd done.

Meg leaned over and rubbed my shoulder. "But at least you know. He doesn't even know."

"Yeah, I guess. I just never want to see him again," I groaned.

"Don't lie, Katie." Meg laughed. "You love him. There's nothing wrong with that, but I do agree. It's time to move on. I think he's being an asshole and he's cheating on his fiancée. He's not a nice guy. Yeah, he has a son and seems to love him, but why would he potentially ruin his family by sleeping with you? He's an egomaniac and a jerk. He likes the power of taking whatever woman he feels like taking. He doesn't seem to care about you at all. I mean, why would he be doing all of this?"

"I just don't get it. I know I lied when we dated. I know I hurt him. But he hurt me too." I sighed. "I don't know why he's still trying to hurt me."

"Maybe you need to have an honest conversation with him. Tell him everything and ask him to let you be. You need to move on, Katie. Meet a new guy. A nice guy."

"I kinda met someone." I made a face. "Well, we kissed."

"What? You met someone and didn't tell me?" Meg looked at me, clearly hurt.

"Just recently. And I'm not really interested in him. He's a bartender at Getting Lucky's. He kinda gave me a kiss and hinted that he'd like to do more."

"Is he hot?"

"He's sexy and hot." I laughed and then sighed. "I just can't think of anyone else that way though."

"Katie, you need to stop letting this guy ruin all your potential relationships. He is not worth it." Meg shook her head. "Have a final conversation with him. End it. And move on."

"Yeah, I guess you're right." I sipped on my wine. "Someone has been texting me all night. Let me see if it's him."

"If it's him, tell me what he said and I will tell you what to text back."

"Argh, okay." I laughed, jumped up, and grabbed my phone. "Okay, here are his texts. First one. 'Hey Katie, I hope you're enjoying your night in. If you want company let me know.'" I laughed. "Sure, Brandon. I'm going to text you right now."

"Read the rest."

"Okay, number two. 'Hey Katie, I sure hope you're not doing anything you're going to regret right now.'"

"What does that mean?" Meg frowned.

"No idea." I shrugged. "Okay, number three. 'Katie, I need you to call me right now.' Number four. 'Katie, text me back or call now.' Number five. 'Katie, stop playing games. Call me now.' Number six. 'Katie, I don't know what the fuck you're doing, but call me now.' What the fuck is his problem?" I groaned, but inside I felt a secret excitement that he wanted to talk to me so badly.

"He is sounding like a psycho." Meg made a face. "What is his problem? He is on such a power trip. Does he expect you to drop everything for him just because he says so?"

"I think he does."

"Yet he can fuck other women and even marry someone else." Meg's voice was passionate. "What an arrogant asshole."

"He said he was going to dump Maria." I stared at her with my heart thudding as I remembered his words. "He said she didn't mean anything to him."

"Did he dump her?" Meg bit her lip. "Not to be mean, but isn't that what they all say? Actions speak louder than words, and to me, it looks like he's just playing a game with you."

34

"I want the truth." I sighed. "And he also said Matt is Maria's brother."

"What the fuck?" Meg's jaw dropped open. "That cannot be a coincidence."

"I don't know." I sipped some more wine. "He fell asleep after sex and then when I woke up he was gone."

"Text him back and tell him you want to see him, but only if he is going to prepare some answers."

"Really?" I frowned. "Maybe I can ask him over the phone."

"No." She shook her head. "You'll know if he's telling the truth by the look in his eyes."

"That's true, I suppose."

"This shit is crazy." Meg yawned. "This is really crazy."

"I told you." I laughed, though I didn't think it was funny. I was about to text Brandon back when my phone rang. "Oh, shit. It's him. Should I answer?"

"No." She shook her head. "Let him wait it out." She smiled evilly. "And actually, don't text him until tomorrow. Let him stew a little bit."

"Oh, Meg." I put the phone on the table and sighed. "Why does life have to be so complicated?"

"Men make it that way." She jumped up and we both laughed as the phone started ringing again. "Let's go to bed. Leave the phone out here, so you aren't tempted to answer."

"Night, Meg." I gave her a quick hug before walking into my room and collapsing onto the bed. I was exhausted, mentally and emotionally, and I fell into a deep, uncomfortable sleep right away.

***

I woke up late the next day, momentarily forgetting that everything was not right in my world. I stretched languorously in the bed and yawned. Even though I'd slept for a long time, I was still tired.

"Katie." Meg knocked on my door. "Are you awake?"

"Yeah," I called out. "Come in."

Meg slowly opened the door and walked into the room. She had a weird look on her face, and I sat up to see what was going on.

35

"What's up?"

"You have a—" She started talking, but then Brandon suddenly appeared behind her.

"Good morning, Katie." His voice was gruff and his eyes looked at me manically. His hair was scruffy and it looked like he hadn't shaved in a couple of days.

"What are you doing here, Brandon?"

"I thought I told you to wait in the living room," Meg said at the same time. Brandon didn't even acknowledge her question or mine as he walked farther into the room and looked around.

"I called you." His voice was accusing. "And I texted you. I told you to call me back."

"I was in bed."

"Sure." His eyes were angry. "How was your early night?"

"It was fine." I blushed and looked at Meg for support. It was so much easier to tell myself to not give a shit, but now he was here in front of me and all I wanted to do was kiss him and pull him down to the bed.

Meg spoke up. "You don't own her. You can't just barge in here and question her."

"Why? Because only lawyers can question?" He looked back at Meg with a sarcastic face. "Or can unemployed lawyers still question?"

"I—oh, you are so rude." Meg glared at him and then at me before striding out of the room. "Thanks for telling him my business."

"I didn't!" I called after her and frowned. "How did you know Meg lost her job?" I narrowed my eyes as I looked at Brandon, who was staring down at me. His nostrils were flaring as he studied my face.

"Where were you last night?" He sat on the bed next to me, pulled the sheets down, and surveyed my body.

"What are you doing?" I pulled the sheets back up.

"I was checking to see if you were wearing any clothes."

"How dare you!" I pushed his chest to get him off of the bed, but he didn't move.

"Oh, I dare all right." He glared at me and his fingers played with my hair. "Your hair looks like you've been through a washing machine. Rough night?"

"My night was fine."

36

"Your lips don't look battered." His fingers traced along my lips and he smiled. "You didn't fuck anyone last night."

"What are you talking about?" I glared at him again.

"Nothing." His eyes glittered at me. "It's nothing I can't fix."

"What are you fixing?"

"I missed you last night." He changed the subject. "I wanted to see you."

"Well, I was busy."

"You're never too busy for me."

"Sorry, but that's not true." I turned away from him. "Why are you here, Brandon?"

"Because I want to make love to you." His fingers gripped my face and turned it toward him so that we were staring into each other's eyes. "My body is craving your touch. My mouth is craving your taste. My fingers and my dick are craving your pussy."

"You're so crude," I mumbled in a daze against his lips. I felt myself growing wet at his words and hated myself for being so intensely attracted to this man.

"I'm not going to make love to you now." His lips pressed against mine and my body melted into him automatically. "I'm not going to suck on your nipples as if they were little candies made for my mouth. I'm not going to eat you like you were a Sunday dinner and I'm not going to take you on a roller coaster ride." He grinned as his fingers played with my hair and I breathed heavily against his lips. "I'm not going to do any of that right now."

"Oh." I couldn't say anything else. His tongue plunged into my mouth and my fingers found his hair as we kissed. We kissed each other eagerly and hungrily, our lips dancing a mambo as our tongues waltzed. He tasted sweet as always, and my fingers ran across the stubble of his face lightly. I moaned as we kissed and I thought about the stubble tickling me in my private place. I wanted him badly. My body couldn't resist his touch.

"Now, now, Katie." He pulled away from me slightly as my fingers worked their way to the front of his pants. "I told you, there will be no sex right now. But tonight, my dear... Tonight is a different story."

"What's going on tonight?" I gazed into his eyes and a little whimper escaped as he cupped my breast.

"Tonight, I'm taking you on a little adventure."

"What adventure?"

"It's a surprise." He grinned at me.

"I'm not going." I shook my head. "We need to talk."

"We can talk, but tonight we will have some fun as well." He grinned at me. "Wear a dress or a short skirt."

"Why?" My heart was beating fast now.

"You'll see." His eyes glittered and he leaned in to kiss me again.

"That's not fair." I shook my head. "You can't just come here and demand I go out with you tonight when you won't tell me where and you won't give me any other information."

"I'll tell you two things." He grinned at me wickedly. "If you do one thing for me?"

"What's that?"

"Ride me," he mumbled against my lips, and I frowned.

"I thought you said no sex."

"I don't want you to ride my cock," he laughed as he squeezed my breasts.

"I don't get it then," I moaned and pushed myself into his hands.

"I want you to ride my face."

"What?" My eyes widened.

"I know you like the stubble." He grinned at me wickedly. "And my tongue. I need to taste you before I leave."

"But what about you?" I whispered, feeling excited.

"I'll come tonight." He laughed and his eyes hardened slightly. "Tonight, you will ride me again. But that time, it will be my cock and I will have the best orgasm of my life."

"I guess." I shivered slightly. "I'm not agreeing to anything until you tell me what you have to say."

"I told you that Matt and Maria are brother and sister, right?"

"Uh huh." I sat up straight and stared at him intently. Was I finally going to get the information I always wanted?

"Their dad, Will, used to work for me. He was a private investigator for my dad's company, and that's how I met him. He was a good guy. He helped me in a lot of ways before I met

38

you and after I met you. He had a heart attack a few years ago."

"I'm sorry."

"It's okay," he sighed. "He left me a note asking me to take care of his daughter, Maria, and to continue supporting his business, which his son, Matt, took over."

"Oh," I frowned. "I thought Matt was a journalist."

"He is a journalist." Brandon sighed. "But he grew up in the family business, so he was able to be a private investigator as well."

"Oh." I was still confused. I didn't really understand how any of it added up.

"Right after her father died, Maria's fiancé dumped her and she attempted to commit suicide." Brandon looked at me with concern in his eyes "Matt came to me and asked me if I would become engaged to her as a way to help her mentally, and I agreed." He sighed. "It was stupid of me. I don't know what I was thinking. We should have just gotten her a therapist. But I figured, what could it hurt? It seemed to make her happy to be in a fake engagement and she didn't demand anything of me."

"So you didn't sleep with her?" I asked slowly, and he nodded.

"I told you I didn't sleep with her." He spoke angrily "I don't love her and we have never had sex. She's not the love of my life."

"So she's not Harry's mother?"

"No." Brandon shook his head and stared at me. I wanted to ask him who was then. Who was the lady he had a kid with? But I was scared and jealous. I didn't want to think about him having a baby with someone else.

"So you don't love Maria?"

"No." He shook his head. "I've never loved her."

"I see." My stomach flipped at his words. Did that mean that I had a shot? Or was I fooling myself? If he found out what I'd done, would he still be interested in seeing me? "So you paid Matt to give you information about me after I started working for you?"

"Something like that." His eyes glazed over. "That's enough talking for now."

"But I wanted to know—" I started, but he placed his finger in my mouth.

39

"Shhh." He grinned as I sucked on it slowly. He pulled the sheets down and pulled me up toward him before pulling his finger out of my mouth. "Come here," he growled as he tore off my t-shirt off and saw that I wasn't wearing a bra or panties. "You make me so hard, Katie."

I laughed at the expression on his face, which seemed to make him happy because he covered me with kisses as he laid down on the bed next to me. He lifted me up gently and placed me on his chest, and I quickly went to undo his belt buckle.

"No." He shook his head as his fingers pushed my ass so that my whole body was closer and closer to his face. "My clothes stay on."

"But," I protested, suddenly feeling self-conscious. I was sitting high on his chest now, my legs spread-eagled on both sides of him. I could feel his breath on my pussy and every part of me was tingling in sweet anticipation.

"No buts." He grinned and then lifted my ass up slightly. I shifted forward onto my knees and hovered over his mouth before looking down to make sure I wasn't smothering him. His eyes sparkled at me before his arms pulled my thighs down roughly and I was sitting directly on his face. My eyes widened for two seconds and then I gripped the headboard as his tongue slowly licked my pussy lips. My body buckled slightly as I felt him sucking on my clit while his stubble gently tickled me. My body started trembling and I moved back and forth on him gently, loving the feel of him against me. I felt his tongue lapping up my wetness before slowly entering me. In that moment his tongue felt just as magnificent as his cock, and I closed my eyes, delighting in the waves of pleasure as they crashed over me. His hands gripped my ass and he slowly moved me back and forth on his face as his mouth devoured me. I screamed as I felt an orgasm overtaking my body. I shuddered on top of him as I came, but Brandon didn't stop licking and teasing me. Instead he increased the motion of his tongue and I moved my hips more urgently on his face as I felt a second orgasm building up.

"Oh, Brandon!" I screamed as I rode his face, forgetting to be gentle. My second orgasm built up even higher, and as the waves of pleasure tore through my body, I almost forgot who I was. I rolled onto the bed next to him and closed my eyes, trying not to move as I lay there feeling satiated and spent. "Until tonight, my love." Brandon jumped off of the bed and kissed me lightly on the cheeks. "I'll see you tonight." He walked out of my room with a confident swagger and I groaned into my pillow. I had no idea what he had planned, but I knew that I was in for one hell of a night.

I smiled to myself as I thought about Brandon and what he had said about Maria and Matt. Maybe I was going to be luckier than I thought. Maybe I was actually in it for a lot longer than one night. I sighed as I thought about everything I had left to tell him. I would tell him all my secrets at the end of the night. And then he could make up his mind once and for all. We were either going to make it work or we weren't. But I couldn't keep going on like this. I would drive myself crazy. I couldn't allow my body and my brain to keep fighting like this. One of them had to win out.

***

"You look hot." Meg attempted a whistle as I exited my bedroom to wait for Brandon.

"So do you." I blinked at her. "Where are you off to?"

"I got a call from the private club." She smiled. "They want me to come in for an interview. The owner is back from some business trip or something."

"Uhm, that doesn't explain the sexy outfit," I laughed.

"I figured men will buy more alcohol from sexy girls." She grinned at me. "I want to show them I can be sexy."

"You're going to go to work like that?"

"No," she giggled. "But they don't need to know that. I'm going to go to the interview like this, and if I get the job, I'll dress regularly. What are they going to say? 'Hey, you bait-and-switched us at the interview'?"

"I guess." I laughed. "You're the lawyer, you know better than me."

"Haha, well, you're the sex queen." Meg's eyes laughed at me. "I need to get some makeup tips from you. You look hot."

"Well, you know. We're not in college anymore." I grinned and paused as we heard a knock on the door.

41

"How does he get up here without us buzzing him in?" Meg looked at me in confusion.

"He owns the building." I made a face.

"And that explains how we got into this building." Meg laughed and shook her head. "I always wondered how we got approved."

"Oh, wow. I never even thought about that." I stared at her, my mind buzzing.

Bang, bang.

"I can hear you girls talking. Don't make me open the door myself." Brandon's voice carried through the door and I walked to open it slowly.

"Hey," I said shyly, grinning at him as his eyes popped open. He stared at my partially exposed breasts and then down to my heavily exposed legs.

"You look amazing." He looked back up at me and I could see the desire in his eyes.

"Amazing enough for you to tell me where we're going?"

He smiled at me and licked his lips as he cocked his head to the side. "Nearly."

"Whatever," I pouted and he laughed.

"Hello, Meg."

"Hi, Brandon." She nodded at him. I could tell she still didn't really like him.

"Where are you off to?"

"A private club." She shrugged. "I've got an interview."

"Oh?" He frowned. "What club?"

"I don't know. It's just called The Club, from what I know."

"The Club?" He stilled and then gave me a quick look. "Hmm. Why are you going to interview there?"

"To get a job as a bartender." She rolled her eyes.

"I thought you were a lawyer."

"Well, I'm taking a break." She pulled on her coat. "And I'm leaving now."

"Wait." Brandon grabbed her arm and paused. "I don't think you should go. If it's the club I'm thinking of, it's not for you."

"I don't need your advice, thanks." She pulled away from him and gave me a smile. "Have a good night, Katie. If you need anything, just call." She gave him a glare. "And if you do anything to hurt my friend, I will cut your balls off." And then she gave him a huge smile and left.

"Well, she doesn't hold back, does she?" He raised an eyebrow at me and I laughed.

"You shouldn't try to tell her what to do. You don't have some special power over every woman, you know."

"I don't?" He winked at me and I hit him in the shoulder.

"How did you know she got fired?" I looked up at him carefully.

"Oh, Katie. Do we have to talk about this now?" He sighed and I nodded. "I know the partners at her old firm. I gave them a call."

"But why?" I held my breath, my heart beating fast.

"I had a feeling you were going to leave the training in San Francisco and quit. I couldn't let that happen. I knew you wouldn't quit if your best friend and roommate had been fired."

"Oh, Brandon." My face paled at his words. Inside I felt both excited and annoyed. How could he have done that to Meg? "She loved that job."

"I'll give them a call next week." His eyes burned into mine. "She'll get her job back."

"Are you sure?"

"Yeah," he nodded. "I don't want her working at the club."

"Why not?"

"If it's the club I'm thinking about, I don't think it's a good idea." His eyes darkened for a moment. "It's not a good idea at all."

"Okay," I shrugged. "So are we going now?"

"Sure, my eager beaver." He laughed and pulled me toward him before kissing me hard. I melted into his chest, and his hands rested lightly on my ass before slowly pulling the back of my dress up. His fingers caressed my ass and he gasped as he realized I had no panties on. "You are a naughty girl."

"I wanted to be accommodating." I grinned and pressed myself into his erection as he growled against my ear.

"I'm going to blindfold you, Katie," He whispered in my ear. "And I'm going to put earmuffs on your ears. I don't want you to see or hear anything. I want every part of your body to be focused on me as you take me."

"As I take you?"

43

"Remember my lap dance fantasy?" he whispered as his fingers teased me. "I want you to pretend you're a stripper and fuck me."

"How can I do that with a blindfold and earmuffs?" I shook my head.

"You'll find a way." He grinned at me. "When we get to the location, I'll kiss you to let you know you can start."

"I don't know." I shook my head. "This sounds awkward."

"Do it for me, Katie." He kissed me again. "I want to own your body tonight. Please me and I will please you."

"Fine." I grinned up at him. "But tomorrow morning, we need to talk. A serious talk. Do you hear me?"

"Fine." He kissed my lips one more time. "Tomorrow we shall talk."

He pulled away from me, took a blindfold out of his pocket, and placed it over my eyes. I was enveloped in darkness and suddenly felt very nervous. I had no idea where we were going, and I didn't know what to expect. He then placed a pair of earmuffs over my ears and all sound was gone as well. I held on to his arm as he escorted me out of the door and into the elevator. I took a deep breath and tried to calm my nerves as we got into the back of a car. Brandon stroked my leg as we drove and I leaned into him. I had no idea where we were going, but I was starting to get excited.

About twenty minutes later, Brandon escorted me out of the back of the car and we walked for about five minutes before he took me into a building. I wasn't even sure where we were and if he was opening any doors or what since we stopped every few seconds for him to do something. Then he picked me up and carried me, and before I knew it, I was being placed on a lush velvet couch. The material was soft underneath me and I wondered if we were in his apartment. I so wanted to pull off the blindfold and the earmuffs, but I knew he would be upset, and part of me enjoyed the thrill of it all. I felt Brandon slide down next to me and his thigh felt warm against mine. I waited in sweet anticipation for him to kiss me, and when it came, I climbed eagerly into his lap.

I straddled him and grinned against his mouth as I felt his erection pressing into me. He kissed me hard and his tongue danced along with the beat of my hips as I gyrated on him. His hands pushed my ass against him harder and I groaned as he broke the kiss and sucked on my neck. I continued moving back and forth on him like I was some sort of dirty stripper and I moaned against his hair as his fingers slipped between my legs. His head then moved farther down my neck until his teeth were pulling the top of my dress to the side. Then I felt his lips on my nipple and I ran my hands to his hair and pulled.

I continued gyrating on him for about a minute before reaching down to let his cock out. It felt hard and long, and I sat up a little bit before sliding down on him and taking him inside of me. His fingers gripped my waist and moved me up and down on him. I cried out as I bounced on top of him and rubbed my breasts in his face. I could feel that he was about to orgasm at the same time I was, and I squeezed his shoulders as he bit down on my nipple. I moved faster and faster and screamed as I climaxed on top of him. I could feel his body shuddering as he came in me and ripped the blindfold off of my face.

My eyes couldn't even focus as my orgasm was so intense, but I soon realized that I was staring into the street. I looked around and realized that not only was I not in Brandon's apartment, I was in a store somewhere, on a couch in the corner of the room. I looked around the dark room and discovered I was in a bar. I could see a couple of people across the way looking at us, and I froze on top of him. Brandon looked down at me with dark eyes and kissed me again as he slipped the earmuffs off. I was about to ask him where we were when I heard a voice behind me.

"I'm going to have to ask you both to leave this instant," a familiar male voice spoke up and I froze. Brandon's hands were still on my waist, holding me down on him, and I was unable to get off of his lap.

"We'll be gone in a moment." Brandon's voice was terse. "I'm sure you understand that it will be better if I finish in her rather than on the couch."

"Dude, if you don't want me to call the cops, you better get out of here." The man's voice was shocked. "You and your girl need to leave my bar now."

And then it hit me. I knew where I was. I twisted my head and saw the Getting Lucky sign on the door. My heart froze as I turned to look at the man who was speaking. It was the bartender from the other night. My face turned red as he stared at me, and his eyes widened in shock.

"Katie." He took a step back and looked at me with a disappointed face.

"I, uh..." I stammered, not knowing what to say.

"We need to go, Katie." Brandon's voice was pleased as his hands released their grip on my waist. He made a show of pulling the back of my dress down and letting his fingers hover on my pussy for a few seconds as he rubbed it gently. His hands then went to the front of my dress and pinched my nipples before adjusting the top. He then slid me off of him and jumped up, pulling me up with him. "This is for your inconvenience." He dropped some bills on the table and nodded at the bartender. "Let's go."

He grabbed my hand and pulled me with him out of the bar. I looked at the ground in shame as we exited quickly. My blood was boiling and I didn't know what to do.

"You're mine, Katie," he whispered in my ear as we left the bar. "I expect you to never come back to this bar." His eyes glittered as he stared at me. "You better not lie to me and see that man ever again."

Chapter 4
Brandon

Katie's eyes were wide with shock and anger, and I knew that I had pushed her too far. I was scared inside, and I knew my jealousy had allowed me to cross a line I shouldn't have.

"How dare you!" She yanked her hand away from me. "Why did you do this?"

"I wanted to show the bartender that he could never have you." The words sounded weak coming from my mouth. I knew that I sounded like some sort of caveman. But I didn't know how to explain to her how much she meant to me and how badly I had hurt the night before when Matt had called me. I'd gone down to the bar after I'd gotten off of the phone with Matt with intentions of letting the bartender know that he needed to back off. But then I'd thought, *What if he takes that as a reason to really start pursuing her?* What if I saw them kissing or doing something even worse? I would have gone crazy. I'd pictured the blood in my mind and had texted and called Katie all night. But she hadn't answered the phone or texted me back. She had all but confirmed my fears, and all I could think of was her with another man, letting him touch her and kiss her. It had driven me crazy. And in my mind, there was only one way for me to make sure that she never hooked up with him. He had to know and she had to know that she was mine.

"Why?" She shook her head and her eyes were devoid of light. "I barely even know him."

"You kissed him!" I almost shouted, feeling angry again as I thought about her lips on his.

"How do you know that?" She paused and her eyes widened. "Are you having me followed?"

"No." I shook my head quickly.

"Then how did you know I knew him?"

"You told me you kissed him. You told me!" I shouted and tried to grab her hands.

"I didn't tell you where I was." She pulled away from me. "Are you some freaking stalker, Brandon? Really, you're a creeper and a stalker."

47

"I know you came here last night as well." I couldn't stop myself. "You told me you were staying in, but you came here to see him again."

"What?" Her mouth dropped open in shock. "How do you know I came here?"

"So you don't deny it?" My heart broke as I realized that Matt hadn't been lying. "You did come here to see him last night."

"I came back last night because I forgot to pay the last time I was here." She looked at me angrily. "'The last time I was here, I ordered a bunch of drinks and ran out because when *he* kissed me, all I could think about was you. I remembered that I hadn't paid, so I came back yesterday to pay what I owed."

"You didn't come back because you wanted him?" My heart beat faster and I grinned at her, happy.

"No, you fucking asshole." Her eyes glittered at me. "You just humiliated me for nothing."

"I'm sorry, I didn't mean to—"

"Oh shut up!" she screamed. "I'm done, you hear? I'm done. I can't take this anymore, Brandon. You use me and treat me like some sort of two-dollar whore. I'm not going to let you do this to me anymore. I don't want to see you ever again. You're a fucking stalker. How dare you have me followed!"

"I didn't have you followed." I grabbed ahold of her. "I swear it. Matt was in here last night and he saw you, and we put two and two together."

"How would he know to put anything together? Why would he even call you and tell you that? Do you know how crazy that sounds, Brandon? My ex-boyfriend called my other ex-boyfriend to tell him that I'm at a bar."

"He said you were flirting."

"So what? I can flirt with anyone I like."

"You kissed him as well." I knew the words sounded childish coming out of my mouth.

"I can kiss him if I want to, Brandon, you don't own me. We're not even together."

"I haven't been with anyone since you, Katie, and I know you haven't either."

"What?" She froze and she stared at me before hitting me in the chest. "How do you know who I have and haven't been

48

with? How long have you been spying on me? Oh my God, Brandon. Are you fucking crazy?"

"Wait." My heart froze at her words. "It's not like that, Katie. I love you."

"No, you don't." She shook her head. "I don't even know if you ever did. You know I never stopped loving you, Brandon. I've been thinking about the man you were when we met and I've dreamed of the day that I would get to see you again. I hoped that we'd be able to move on from what happened seven years ago. I thought that if I saw you again, and you saw me, we would have another connection. And yeah," she laughed hysterically, "I looked you up and tried to see what you were up to and who you dated. And yeah, I bumped into Matt on purpose because I wanted to know more about you. I wanted to be around you again and see if we had a shot at another chance. What I did was wrong. I snooped and I did things I'm ashamed of. But I did it because I thought I loved you. I did it because I thought that maybe we still had a shot."

"We do! We—" I started, but she cut me off.

"But you're not the man I thought you were, Brandon. I thought you were strong and kind and compassionate. I thought you were loving and protective. But you're not. You're just a fucking asshole, like every other man who's on a power trip. Well, you know what? You can fuck off. I'm done. You can't tell me who I can and can't fuck. If I want to go back into the bar and fuck the bartender now, I will. And you can't stop me. Do you hear me? I'm not your possession. You do not own me. You cannot humiliate me and tell me you think it's okay because you were jealous. That's not how life goes, Brandon. At least not for me."

She stared at me for a moment, and I watched as tears fell down her face. It reminded me of the day we had broken up when she was at Columbia University. I stood still as she stared at me waiting for me to speak, but I didn't know what to say.

She turned around and walked away, and I watched her hobbling. I felt sick to my stomach at what I'd done and at her words. She didn't love me anymore. I'd pushed her too far. It was over. A part of me was resigned to watching her leave. This was my life and my destiny. I was meant to be alone.

As I watched her walk away, I thought back to that day seven years ago. The day that created a cut in my heart so deep that I was sure it would never be repaired. I remembered standing in the front of the class, waiting for her to look up and see me. I'd seen her right away—I had some sort of Katie sensor that knew where she was immediately whenever she was near me. Her eyes had widened in shock and fear as she glanced at me.

I was surprised that I had been able to keep it together as I gave my speech. I knew as I spoke to the group of eager freshmen that it was over. I'd given her so many chances, but she'd proven to me that she wasn't ready. My heart had broken when she'd thought we still had a chance, when she'd thought I'd forgiven her for her duplicity.

I hadn't wanted to hurt her or to break her. I just wanted her to feel the pain I had felt. I'd given her so many chances, and she had never come through. While I fucked her over the dumpster, I felt like a sick fuck. A perverted wannabe. I wanted her to scream and to shout at me then. I wanted her to realize why I had to do what I did. She was too young. She didn't know the world and she didn't know her own mind.

So I'd fucked her and walked away and then I'd watched her collapse onto the ground in tears. And I'd just walked away with my heart in my mouth and my head pounding with hate.

I waited for her to show up the next day, to tell me she was sorry and that she loved me and wanted to make it work. But she never came back. She never called and I never called and that was it. The end. It was so easy and simple and it was as if we'd never been together. Only the hole in my heart never grew back.

I'd hired Will to follow her and keep an eye on her. Not every day, but just to make sure everything was okay. He reported back to me once a week and I would read his reports and study his photographs while lying on the bed and staring at a photograph we'd taken together on a trip to the museum. When Will told me that he thought she was sick, I nearly called her. Enough was enough. I couldn't stand back while the love of my life was sick. But then Will got the hospital records and I found out the truth. At first I was excited and then a little scared. I knew she would call me then. How could she not? I knew I could have called, but I wanted her to reach out first. I wanted her to make the decision that she wanted to be with me because she loved me. I didn't want her to feel trapped. She was so young, and I didn't want to be the guy who did that. But she never called, and my world grew bleaker and darker. She never called and I never called, and eventually it was over and both of our lives had changed. I'd hated her and loved her, both at the same time.

As I stood there watching her walk away again, tears running down her face, I knew that I couldn't make the same mistake twice. This time, I was going to fight for her. This time, I wasn't going to just let her go. I wasn't perfect—I knew that. But I still loved her, and I had to try again.

"Wait!" I shouted as I ran after her. I grabbed ahold of her shoulders and stopped her. "Wait a minute."

"What?" She looked at me coldly and I took a deep breath before speaking again.

"I know you don't want to see me again. I understand that."

"Good." She glared at me and shook my hand off of her shoulder.

"But what about your son?" I paused as her face turned white. "Do you want to see your son?"

"What are you talking about?" she whispered, and I grabbed her arms to keep her from falling.

"I know you were pregnant, Katie." I stared into her wide eyes. "I don't know how you could give him up without telling me, but I know."

"I, I..." She blinked rapidly and her eyes glazed over. "I'm sorry I didn't tell you."

"I understand why." I pulled her toward me. "You were young. You didn't know what to do. I understand."

"Do you hate me?" Tears started flowing from her eyes again. "I'm sorry I never told you. I didn't know what to do after what happened, and then I found out I was pregnant. I was so scared. I was just eighteen and a freshman. I had no one to turn to."

"I could never hate you, Katie." I rubbed the back of her head. "I shouldn't have ended things the way that I did."

"I've always regretted it, you know." Her eyes glazed over. "I wish I'd kept him. He would have been a piece of you that I would have always had. He's still in my heart."

51

"I know."

"I love him," she cried. "I hate you, Brandon. I hate you for doing this to me."

"I'm sorry, Katie. I made a mistake." I sighed. "I've made a lot of mistakes. And I'm sorry about tonight. You have to believe that. You have to believe me. Please. I didn't mean to hurt you. I can't live without you."

"I don't know what to say." She shook her head as if to clear it.

"You don't have to say anything. I'm not going to force you to give me another chance. I'm not going to predicate anything on our getting back together." I took a deep breath. I couldn't lose her again.

"I don't know what you want, Brandon."

"I don't want anything. Do you want to meet Harry?"

"Harry?" She gave me a weird look.

"He's your son, Katie." I stared down at her and smiled. "Harry's our son." Katie's eyes gazed at me in confusion, before she finally understood what I was saying. I held on tightly to her as she collapsed into my arms in shock.

Chapter 5
Katie

Sleep eluded me as I lay in bed. I stared at the clock on the nightstand and sighed. It was four a.m. I still had four hours before Brandon was going to pick me up and take me to meet Harry.

"Harry," I said slowly in the dark. "Harry," I said again and smiled. I was going to meet my son. My son.

It didn't even seem real. I was scared and I was excited, both at he same time. He was a little over six years old now. My heart broke as I thought about the six years of his life I had lost. Six years I would never get back. Six years Brandon had devoted to him. Our son.

I didn't know how to think about Brandon anymore. I still loved him; I knew I probably would always love him. But I wasn't sure I could deal with his style of crazy. He was too hard for me to figure out and his actions were too extreme. I cringed as I thought about the incident in the bar. I could still remember the hot burn on my face as I had made eye contact with the bartender. He had looked disgusted and shocked, so different than the teasing sweetness of the previous two days.

What Brandon had done was unacceptable. But his revelation after the incident had taken my breath away. I couldn't believe that he had known all this time that we'd had a baby. That he was now raising our baby. My hand flew to my mouth as I cried out. He wasn't a baby anymore. I didn't have a baby. He was a young boy. I'd missed the first years of his life. I felt tears forming in my eyes as I thought about everything I'd lost.

Beep beep.

My phone went off and I grabbed it quickly.

"Hey." It was Brandon.

I texted back quickly. "Hey."

"What are you doing?"

"Sleeping."

"Want to talk?"

"No."

"I can't sleep."

"That sucks for you."

"I'm thinking about what an ass I am."

"Good for you."

"My fingers are getting tired typing. Can I call you?"

I lay there staring at the phone. I wanted to talk to him, but I didn't.

"Did I lose you? :(" he texted back again and I smiled.

"No, I'm still sleep-texting."

"I knew you were smart :)"

"I did go to Columbia, you know!"

"I know. A little birdie told me."

"Haha."

"What are you wearing?"

"Nothing."

"What? I want a photo."

"I meant none of your business."

"Not fair."

"What are you wearing?" I shook my head as I typed.

"Boxers."

"Oh."

"I can send you a pic if you want! :) :)"

"I don't want."

":("

I snuggled into the sheets and smiled as I waited for his next text. I held the phone in my hands eagerly and felt my smile fade as I realized that he might not text me back again.

Beep beep.

"Miss me yet?"

"No." I smiled to myself again.

"You have to admit that it was slightly hot."

"It was not hot." I glared at the phone.

"I made you come."

"You always make me come!"

"Score 1 for me. :)"

"Idiot."

"I love you."

"I'm going back to sleep now. Bye." I put the phone down and closed my eyes. My heart was beating fast as I thought about his words. I picked the phone back up and stared at the screen. I didn't know what to think or feel. Did he really love me?

Then the phone rang and I bit my lower lip. I didn't know whether or not I should answer.

"I thought you weren't going to answer." His voice was soft as he spoke into the phone.

"I guess you thought wrong," I whispered into the phone and closed my eyes.

"You sound sexy when you're sleeping."

"Really?" I giggled and faked a snore.

"That's even sexier."

"You're not allowed to call me sexy."

"Is it too soon?"

"Huh?"

"I guess I'm still in trouble. I'll save the sexy talk for next week."

"You'll still be in trouble next week, Brandon." I shook my head. "I'm still mad at you."

"You can't stay mad at me."

"You think?"

"I hope." His voice was warm and husky. "I wish I were with you right now."

"So you can make love to me again?"

"No. So I can hold you in my arms and kiss you."

"Uh huh."

"And smell you."

"Smell me?" I frowned and lifted my arm up to see if my armpit smelled.

"You always smell like gardenias." I could hear the smile in his voice.

"Really?" I sniffed again and all I could smell was a faint sniff of the popcorn I'd made when I got home.

"Yeah. When I'm with you, I feel like I'm home."

"Oh." My heart melted at his words. "I'm still mad at you."

"I'm excited for you to meet, Harry." His tone changed. "I think you'll like him."

"I'm a bit scared," I admitted honestly. "What if he doesn't like me?"

"He'll like you," Brandon laughed. "Don't be scared."

"I've never been around little kids before," I mumbled, though that wasn't what was worrying me. I was scared that I wouldn't feel anything for him. I was scared I would see him and it would be as if I were looking at just another child. And even worse, I was scared we wouldn't have any sort of connection.

"You will be a natural."

"I hope so." I yawned.

"I should let you sleep." Brandon sounded sad. "It's late."

"Just a few more minutes," I mumbled, not wanting to get off of the phone as yet.

"You never answered me, you know," he said.

"Answered what?"

"I told you I loved you." He sounded unsure of himself. "You didn't say anything."

"I didn't know what to say," I answered honestly, feeling confused.

"You think I'm a jerk." He sighed. "I'm not perfect, Katie. I've made my mistakes."

"You can say that again." I rolled my eyes in the dark at his words and turned over in the bed.

"I'm glad you answered the phone." His voice was soft again. "I needed to hear your voice tonight. I couldn't sleep. I needed to know you would still talk to me."

"I don't hate you, Brandon." I sighed. "I just don't want anything from you."

"You think I'm an egomaniac."

"I know you're an egomaniac."

"I suppose it doesn't help if I tell you I want to make you come."

"What?" I gasped into the phone.

"I want you to fall asleep thinking about me inside of you." His voice was silky. "I want to make you come."

"Well, it's a pity you're not here," I murmured into the phone as I imagined him kissing my neck. I let out a little whimper as I imagined him playing with my breasts at the same time.

"What are you doing?" His voice was alert and I knew he had heard my whimper.

"Nothing."

"Play with yourself for me."

"No." I shook my head, but my hands rubbed my stomach.

"I'm thinking about you right now," He whispered into the phone. "I'm imagining your hands soft and cold on my cock, gliding up and down slowly, trying to tease me. I'm imagining your mouth taking over for your hands and your lips sucking down on me, tasting me and biting me lightly." He groaned and I froze as I listened to him.

"What are you doing?" I whispered, waiting for him to continue. His talk was making me feel horny and I shifted in the bed uncomfortably.

"Nothing," he groaned. "It can wait."

"Okay." I was disappointed that he had stopped before he had really gotten started.

"I'm not going to have phone sex with a girl who's sleeping," he joked into the phone. "I want you to remember me in the morning."

"Uh huh."

"But don't worry, it will be your face I picture when we get off the phone."

"What?" I squeaked out.

"Nothing, beautiful Katie," he sighed. "Get some sleep. I'll be picking you up in a few hours."

"Okay," I sighed, not wanting to get off of the phone.

"What's wrong?" he questioned me and I was quiet. "Katie."

"Nothing."

"Do you want me to stay on the phone?" he whispered.

"No," I lied.

"I remember when we first started dating. You always wanted me to stay on the phone with you." He laughed. "I'm not sure how either of us got anything done with all those marathon calls."

"We didn't have that many," I giggled as I remembered those first days.

"We spoke on the phone every night. You talked my ear off going on about books and TV shows." He laughed. "But it was all worth it when I heard your sweet little snores as you fell asleep."

"I don't snore."

"I'm afraid you do."

"No one has ever told me I snored," I protested.

"How many men have you slept with?" His tone changed, and I could hear the jealousy. I felt all warm inside as he spoke and I knew that I was just as dysfunctional as him.

"I'm not answering the question."

"I know the answer already," he laughed.

"You're a creep."

"I didn't stop you from dating anyone."

"I know," I sighed. "Do you ever think about the days before we broke up? The days before I moved in? The first days?"

"All the time."

"They were good, weren't they?"

"The very best."

"Thank you for taking Harry," I whispered.

"I love you, Katie." His voice was stronger this time. "And I love Harry more than life itself."

"You're a good dad."

"I got one thing right." He sighed. "Stay the night tomorrow."

"No."

"Think about it."

"Okay, I'll think about it."

"Sweet dreams, Katie."

"Sweet dreams, Brandon." I waited for him to hang up before I put down the phone. "You're still there," I whispered, and he laughed.

"I'm hoping I get to hear the snores of an angel again."

"You want me to fall asleep on the phone?"

"I want you to fall asleep in my arms, but the phone will have to do tonight."

"Night, Brandon." I closed my eyes and snuggled into my pillow, the phone pressed against my ear. I lay there listening to the sound of his breathing and it comforted me. Before I knew it, I had fallen into a deep sleep and I had dreams filled with Brandon, me, and babies.

***

"Don't worry, Katie. It'll be fine." Brandon squeezed my hand as we walked up to the front door of his dad's house. "Just remember, don't tell him you're his mom, please. I don't want to shock him."

"I won't tell him." I nodded. I felt hurt that Brandon didn't want Harry to know right away, but I understood slightly. "Who does he think Maria is to him?" I frowned as we waited at the door.

"He's only known Maria for the last year or so. She moved in fairly recently." Brandon sighed. "He thinks she's his babysitter."

"Oh." I bit my lower lip to stop from saying anything else.

"Hello," a sweet older lady said when she answered the door. She had platinum blond hair and a big red smile. "Brandon, you're here early." She gave him a hug and then looked at me. "This is my friend Katie, Verna." He introduced us, and the lady known as Verna looked me over with knowing eyes.

"Katie, this is my father's girlfriend, Verna."

"Nice to meet you." I reached over to shake her hand, but she gave me a hug instead.

"It's wonderful to meet you, my girl." She smiled at me happily. "You have such pretty brown eyes."

I smiled back at her, appreciating her warmth to me, and was about to speak when I saw a little boy darting to the door.

"Daddy!" He ran into Brandon's arms, grinning. "I'm having pancakes."

"I can see that," Brandon replied with a smile, and we all laughed as Harry's face was covered in syrup.

"Do you want some pancakes, Dad?" Harry grinned and then looked at me. "Hello, I'm Harry."

"Hi, Harry. I'm Katie." I choked up slightly. "It's nice to meet you."

"Do you like to play video games?" He studied my face for a few moments.

"I'm not terribly good, but I do enjoy some."

"Then come and play Mario Kart with me. It's fine 'cause Granddad said I could play," he quickly added as he looked at his dad, and I laughed. I tried not to stare at him like a crazy woman, but I couldn't stop myself from studying him.

He was a gorgeous little boy and looked like a mini-Brandon but with my big brown eyes. His hair was dirty blond and he had a round little face that looked very dirty at the moment. Though I had a feeling that his face was always slightly dirty. His cheeks were rosy and red and he was a little plump, with his round little belly—probably from playing too many video games.

"Or we could play basketball or soccer." I smiled at him, thinking that it was time to introduce some sports into his life. I

59

laughed inside at my maternal instincts and I saw Brandon giving me a side stare.

"I want to play basketball!" He jumped up and down. "I wanna be just like Kobe Bryant when I grow up."

"Oh?" I nodded at him and smiled. "He's a good player, all right." I knew the name, but I had no idea what basketball team he played for, and I was praying that Harry wouldn't ask me.

"Or LeBron James." He grinned. "I could be LeBron James as well."

"Well, right now you're going to be the little boy who goes and cleans his face." Brandon interrupted us and we all walked into the house. "Go and get cleaned up, Harry. Katie and I are taking you out."

"YES!" He pumped his fist. "McDonalds time."

"No, Harry." He shook his head and laughed. "I thought we could all go to a museum or something."

"Boring." Harry made a face. "I don't wanna go to a museum."

"Don't be rude." Brandon gave him a small stare and I turned my face away to stop from laughing. Brandon was a wonderful father, but it was a bit weird watching him in that role.

"I'm being honest." Harry shrugged and smiled at me. "You know that, right, Katie?"

"Yes, I do think you're being honest."

"See." He grinned at his dad.

"What would you like to do, Harry?" I asked him softly, and he turned to look at me with big adoring eyes. I thought my heart melted right then and there.

"I wanna go McDonalds and to a movie and maybe to a toy store to get some new Legos or a new game for my Wii. And then I wanna go and get some candy." He paused for a second. "But not Reese's Pieces. I don't like Reese's.

"Neither do I," I laughed happily, and Brandon gently smiled at me.

"He favors his mother in a lot of ways," He whispered in my ear. "Brown eyes, doesn't like Reese's, likes to have his own way too much." I gave him a quick look and he grinned at me before turning back to our son. "Harry, go and get cleaned up and come back downstairs please."

"Yes, Dad." Harry ran off and Verna turned to us both.

"You make a lovely couple." She smiled but walked off before I was able to deny he comment.

"She thinks we're together," I groaned and looked at Brandon.

"So?" He shrugged.

"But we're not."

"Yet." He smiled slowly and pulled me toward him. He kissed me lightly on the nose and then on the lips. "I enjoyed falling asleep with you last night."

"Uh huh." I blinked up at him, my heart beating fast.

"Falling asleep with someone is so much more intimate than having sex with them," he whispered in my ear.

"You think so?" I smiled up at him. "Then I guess you never want to have sex with me again?"

"Don't be funny," he laughed as his hands caressed my ass. "If we weren't in my dad's house right now, I'd be fucking you right here."

"Really?" I raised an eyebrow. "And it's only because we're in your dad's house? I thought you got off on public sex."

"Argh." He groaned and his hands massaged my shoulders. "Okay, I'd fuck you here in a minute if Harry weren't here."

"I knew it."

"Does it make you feel better that you're right?" he whispered against my lips, and I leaned in and kissed him hard; this time I was going to turn him on in an awkward place. I slipped my tongue into his mouth and nibbled on his lower lip before pressing my breasts against his chest and reaching down and squeezing his hardening cock.

"Shit, Katie," he groaned against me as I unzipped him, slipped my hand inside his pants, and ran my fingers lightly over his cock. He gasped at my touch and I smiled as I continued to kiss him. As soon as I heard footsteps coming, I withdrew my hand and walked over to look at some paintings on the wall.

"Ready!" Harry ran back to the entryway and I smiled at him widely as Brandon quickly zipped himself back up.

"Well, that was fast, Son." Brandon's voice was tight, and he gave me a look filled with such lust and desire that my panties grew wet.

"Let's go play." Harry grabbed my hand. "Bye, Grandpa. Bye, Grandma Verna."

"Where's your dad?" I asked Brandon, surprised I hadn't met him.

"I think he's still in bed." He laughed. "Verna spoils him and serves him breakfast in bed every morning."

"Oh, wow."

"Let's go." Harry pulled me towards the front door.

"Don't squeeze Katie's hand off, Harry," Brandon chuckled as we walked through the front door.

"I'm not." He laughed and smiled up at me. "I'm not hurting you, am I, Katie?"

"No, Harry." I smiled down at him with love in my eyes. "You're not hurting me at all."

***

"Go up and have a bath, Harry. I'll be up in fifteen minutes to read you a bedtime story."

"Yes, Dad." Harry yawned and looked over at me. "Will I see you tomorrow, Katie?"

"If you want to." I smiled at him happily. We'd had a long day, taking him to a children's museum and then to a late lunch and back home to watch a movie together. It had been such a great day. I was a little sad that it was over.

"Yeah, let's go to McDonalds tomorrow."

"I don't know about McDonalds," I laughed, "but I'm sure we can think of something to do."

"Okay." Harry ran up the stairs, and Brandon came and sat next to me on the couch.

"You're good with him." He stared into my eyes. "You make a good mother."

"I don't know about all that." I made a face and looked around the living room. "I love your house. I didn't know you had a brownstone."

"I bought it after I got Harry." He shrugged. "I still have the apartment though. It's still intact from the days we lived together."

"How did you get Harry?" I bit my lip, but I couldn't stop myself from asking the question that had been on my mind for so long.

"The adoption agency told me it was a closed adoption, but a couple in Connecticut were adopting him."

"The lady in charge of the adoption agency is an advocate for fathers' rights." His voice was low. "I went in and told her that I was the father and they didn't have my permission. We got a blood test done and I took him home."

"They can do that?"

"When you have money, you can get a lot of things pushed through quickly." He shrugged. "I wasn't going to let my son be raised by strangers."

"You think I'm horrible, don't you?"

"No, you were just young." He shook his head and sat back. "There are so many things I think we both would have done differently if we had it to do over." He sighed. "I think that you never really realize what you've lost until it's gone." He stared at me sadly. "Sometimes, the biggest revenge is showing someone what they could have had."

"I don't know what to say." I looked away from him, my heart breaking.

"It was always you, Katie. It was only you. There's never been anyone in my life that I've wanted before. Never." He sighed and stood up. "I wish you hadn't lied to me." His eyes looked down at me and he walked away. "I'm going to go and read Harry a bedtime story now. Feel free to relax until I get back."

I sat back and stared at the rug, feeling as if I were in Wonderland. My emotions were all over the place and I didn't know which way was up and which way was down. I heard footsteps and looked up, expecting to see Brandon, but a tall, beautiful lady walked into the room instead.

"Hello," I smiled at her politely.

"You're a fool." The lady's eyes surveyed me with pity.

"Excuse me?" I sat up straight.

"I said you're a fool, Katie Raymond."

"And you are?" I asked slowly, though I was pretty sure I knew the answer.

"I'm Brandon's fiancée, Maria." She sat next to me. "I'm sure you've heard of me before."

"You were engaged to him in college as well." I nodded, letting her know I did know exactly who she was.

"College?" She laughed. "I'm not that Maria. I'm the new and better version. At least that's what Brandon tells me. The girl in college was a mistake. Like you." She cackled as she looked at me, flinging her long, dark hair behind her shoulders.

"I see." I looked away from her, not knowing what to say.

"When you fucked him, did he say my name?" Maria leaned towards me and hissed. "Did he tell you that he likes to fuck me in the car, in the shower, in the elevator, in the kitchen?"

"He told me he's never slept with you." I jumped up, angry and upset. I wanted to be away from this woman. "He told me he doesn't love you, that he only became engaged to you because of your dad."

Maria started laughing, but I could see her face turning red. "I suppose he's right about one thing. The only woman he ever really loved was Denise."

"Who?" I frowned and turned to look at her.

"Denise. She's the one who ruined him. The one he wishes every woman was like. She was a freak in the bedroom, let him do things to her that other women wouldn't even think of." Maria stood up and smiled at me. "I suppose I should feel sorry for you. You're like me. You got caught up in his lies and his spell. He doesn't love you, you know. This is just about revenge and power for him. He uses us because his true love, Denise, used him. Once you submit to him, he will be gone. Just like he was before."

"You're lying." I turned away from her, not wanting to hear anything else she had to say.

"Go to his study, turn on the TV, and press play on the DVD player." Maria shrugged and turned away from me. "He goes to his study every day and watches that video to remind himself of who he was and what he lost."

"I'm not going anywhere."

"Are you scared, little girl?" She laughed hysterically and then turned around abruptly. I watched as she left the room and the house. I stood there in shock. What was she talking about? I'd never heard of a Denise before in my life. I thought back to the last few weeks and everything that had happened. It had seemed like Brandon had been deliberately trying to humiliate me and hurt me. How did I know if he really truly loved me or if this was just a game to him?

I walked to the study slowly, ashamed of myself for believing Maria's lies. *I just need to know that it's a lie,* I told myself as I

entered the study and turned on the TV. It took me a few
minutes to find the DVD player. It was hidden behind some
books. I pressed play and waited.

The screen flashed on and I blinked. It was Brandon's bedroom
in his apartment that I was looking at—the apartment I had
shared with him. I stared at the screen and watched as
Brandon walked in with two girls. My heart started thudding as I
watched him undressing one while the other one undressed
him. I felt like I couldn't breathe when they all fell to the bed
together. One girl started kissing him while the other went down
on him. I stumbled back until I fell into a chair, but my eyes
didn't move from the screen. I watched as he played with both
girls and teased them. Then one of the women left the room
and it was just him and a tall blonde. A beautiful, voluptuous
blonde. She sat on top of him, teasing him, and he was
groaning as he played with her breasts.

"Fuck me, Denise," he groaned. "Fuck me now." She whispered
something to him and he groaned again. "You know it's always
been you, Denise. I don't want anyone else but you. Please,
just fuck me." His hands reached to her hips and I watched as
she sank down on him and rode him hard. Brandon's eyes
were closed and he muttered something incomprehensible.

"Katie, where are you?" I heard Brandon's voice calling out to
me from the hallway, but I couldn't speak. My tears were
streaming down my face too quickly. A sob escaped from my
mouth and I heard Brandon's footsteps walking towards the
study.

"Katie?" He opened the door slowly. "What's wrong?"
His eyes widened in concern as he stared at me. I pointed to
the TV screen as I couldn't make eye contact with him, and I
heard him gasp.

"What the fuck?" He walked over to the screen and frowned as
he turned it off. "How did you find this?"

"Maria told me to come in and watch it," I gulped.

"Maria was here?" He sighed and walked up to me. "That was
an old video, Katie. Please don't cry. Denise was someone I
knew before I met you."

"She was the love of your life." I tried not to let him see how
much I was breaking inside. "You told her you wanted her and
that she was the one."

"Katie, you have to believe me when I say that Denise was never the one." He shook his head angry. "I could kill Matt."

"Matt?" I looked at him and frowned.

"He must have given Maria the video." He sighed. "He's the only one with access to it, now that his father is dead."

"I don't understand."

"Katie," he sighed. "I didn't want to go into this. But before I met you, I dated a girl called Denise. She was beautiful and sexually adventurous. She liked to have a good time and so did I."

"You guys had threesomes?" I stared at him with accusing eyes and he nodded.

"I told you when I met you, Katie. I wasn't a saint. I'm a virile man. I like sex." He shrugged. "It was all before you." He sighed and then continued. "Anyways, it turned out that Denise was a high-class escort and she had targeted me with some of her colleagues. They tried to blackmail me for twenty million dollars. They were going to go to a newspaper and write a tell-all about all the kinky prostitute sex I liked." My eyes widened as he told his story and he looked at me with a sad expression. "I mean, it was true. The only part that would have been omitted was that I knew they were prostitutes. But no one would have believed me." He crouched down and grabbed my hands. "So I hired a private detective to investigate them. That was how I met Will. When I met you, I really liked you, but I didn't know if I could trust my gut instincts, so I had Will follow you too. In fact, I had him follow both of us. I wanted to know what you did when you were with me and when you weren't with me, so I could be sure that you were genuine."

"I never knew that." My eyes widened, but my tears had dried up.

"I didn't want you to know." He stood up and pulled me up next to him. "You passed with flying colors. Will loved you. He thought you were perfect. His report told me you were the furthest thing from a gold digger he'd seen." He smiled at me gently. "He had just confirmed what I had already known in my heart, Katie. I'm sorry I did it. But you have to know that you are the only one I've truly loved, not Denise. Never Denise. She's nothing to me."

"Liar." We both jumped as Maria walked back into the room with an evil smile. "You're a liar, Brandon Hastings."

"Get out of here." Brandon's face was red with anger. "After all I've done for your family, you try and ruin my life."

"You're a liar, Brandon," Maria hissed as she walked up the TV and turned it on again. She rewound the DVD and pressed play. I cringed as I watched Brandon on the screen moaning in ecstasy with Denise on top of him. "Look carefully, Katie." She pointed at the screen. "For just one moment, stop thinking about your little girl pain and Brandon fucking another woman. Look at the room, Katie. What do you see?"

I tried to ignore her words, but I couldn't. I looked at the room more carefully to see what she was talking about. And then I gasped. I stared at Brandon, angry and hurt. He had lied to me. Everything had been a lie. One great big lie.

"You lied," I whispered, horrified and heartbroken. He stared back at me with an ashen face and I knew then that he knew he had been caught. I turned back to the screen and watched as Brandon made love to another woman with the photograph we'd taken together at the museum staring down at him from the night table next to the bed.

Chapter 6
Brandon

I stared at Katie in dread. She'd caught me in a lie. A big lie. A lie that was more harmful than the lie she'd told me. A lie that meant I'd have to reveal everything if I was to stand a chance of gaining her total trust and love again.

"Nothing to say, Brandon?" Maria's voice was catty and delighted, and I knew that she had deliberately set this whole thing up to hurt me for ending the fake engagement.

"You need to leave. Now." I turned toward her with murder in my eyes.

"I think someone needs to protect poor, innocent Katie. Don't you, Brandon?" She laughed. "We wouldn't want her thinking this was all her fault, would we?" Her eyes narrowed at me and I grabbed her arm.

"You are to leave and never come back." I looked down at her and whispered, "If I ever see you again, I will ruin your brother's life. I will make sure he is fired from the *Wall Street Journal* and is never employed by another newspaper in New York again."

"You wouldn't do that." Her face paled at my words. I knew I had hit a sore spot. She loved her brother Matt more than anyone in the world.

"Don't test me." I pushed her toward the door. "Leave now."

"What about Harry?" She looked at me with big eyes. "He'll miss me."

"You will never see him again." I clenched my fists as I thought about all the times I'd left him alone with her. I wanted to punch myself for being so blind as to how crazy she was.

"But you love me, Brandon," she whimpered. "You wanted to marry me."

"Maria." My voice rose and she ran out of the room. I followed her out and watched as she exited before slowly going back into the room. "I guess I'll have to change the locks," I joked as I re-entered the study, but Katie didn't smile.

I stood there, not knowing what to say or where to start.

"I guess we should talk." I cleared my throat and stared at her. I was surprised to see that she wasn't crying. "I'm sorry for lying."

"One lie begets another lie, I suppose." Her face was expressionless, and my heart froze at the lack of emotion in her tone. I could have dealt with anger, jealousy, or hurt, but her lack of caring scared me.

"I didn't mean to lie." I sighed. "I really didn't want her. I never loved her."

"You slept with her while you were with me?" Katie looked at me curiously. "So you cheated on me?"

"Never." I shook my head vehemently. "It was after."

"After what?"

"We broke up." I took a deep breath. "It was the day you gave Harry up."

"What?" She frowned at me. "That doesn't make sense."

"The day you gave Harry up was the day I realized you were never coming back to me. It was the day I realized you hated me so much that you would have our child and give him up for adoption and never even tell me that I had a son." I stared at her through bleak eyes. "I hated you so much on that day. I hated you and I hated me and I resorted to something I'm not proud of."

"But she blackmailed you." She looked at me with a dazed expression. "Why would you sleep with her?

"Because I hated her as much as I hated myself." I shrugged. "I just needed a body—bodies. I just needed to be out of myself. To forget you and what we'd had. I needed to be with someone and use their body without care for their feelings."

"You did that to me as well." Her voice was soft.

"Never, Katie. I've never used you." I shook my head. "I love you."

"You don't know the meaning of love." She shook her head and closed her eyes. "All these years, I've been berating myself for doing something so stupid, for lying and losing the love of my life, but I think I should have been congratulating myself. I wasn't dumb. I was smart. You're crazy. You're self-obsessed. You only care about yourself. You're not capable of love."

"I love Harry, Katie. I'm a good father." My voice was terse.

"Yes." She nodded slowly. "You're a good father. A very good father."

"Can you forgive me, Katie?"

"There's nothing to forgive." She shrugged. "We both made mistakes. I think it's time we moved on. I want to be in Harry's life if you let me. I want him to know me as his mother."

"You're not going to run away?" I looked at her consideringly. "Now that you know everything, you're not going to leave and never look back like you did seven years ago?"

"No." She looked at me with clear eyes and smiled weakly. "I love my son. I won't ever leave him again. I'm not going to back down this time. I'm not going anywhere."

I fell back against the wall and burst into tears. I couldn't believe it. I couldn't believe that everything was working out the way I had dreamed it would. Katie stared at me in shock, and I walked over to her and pulled her into my arms, kissing the top of her head.

"What are you doing?" She pulled away from me. "Stop it. What's going on, Brandon?"

I walked back to the TV and turned it on again. "Look at the screen," I told her. "Look very carefully."

She looked at me in shock, and I pointed at the image of me. "Look at the face. Look carefully, Katie." She stared at the screen for a few minutes and gasped.

"That's not you." Her face turned ashen as she realized the truth. "What is going on? That's not you!"

"Matt helped me put this video together." I walked over to her and grabbed her hand. "Let's go upstairs." We walked upstairs to my bedroom and I took her to sit down on the bed. "Maria went crazy when I ended things with her. He called me to warn me that he thought she was going to do something crazy. We have this video because, when I refused to pay Denise a dime, she hired someone who was my lookalike to pretend he was me. She took him to my apartment when I was out of town and set up a secret camera to record it. This was going to be her proof to the world." I shook my head. "I told you, she was crazy."

"How did you get it?" Katie looked like she didn't quite believe me.

"Matt got wind of it from a reporter he knows." I shrugged. "He pretended to be interested as a reporter, bought the video, and made her sign non-disclosure papers. It's been locked up for years, but Maria found it recently and well, I guess she decided to try and use it against me."

"That's crazy." Katie looked down at her lap, and I knew that now was the time that I had to let her know how I felt and what was in my heart.

"It's always been you, Katie. Don't you realize that? From the first day I met you, my heart has belonged to you. It's never gone anywhere else. I've just been waiting for you to come back to me."

"I don't know what to believe anymore." She shook her head and sighed. "Why didn't you try and get me back when we broke up? How could you do that to me?"

I grabbed her hands and stared into her eyes. "You were only eighteen, so young. I didn't want to trap you into a relationship if you weren't ready. I wanted it to be you who came to me. I wanted you to realize that I was the man of your dreams. The man you wanted to spend the rest of your life with. I waited so patiently, Katie. Every day, I sat by the phone, waiting. I didn't want to be the man who stole your youth if you weren't ready. When Will told me you were pregnant, I thought, 'This was it. This is when she's going to come back to me. She loves me and she's having my baby. There's no way she's not going to come back.' But you never did. When I heard you were giving away the baby—our baby—I hated you. I couldn't believe that you would give away a part of us. But eventually, I understood why. And I went and got him. And we've just been waiting for you to grow up and come back to us."

"I didn't know what to do. I wanted to tell you, Brandon. I really did. I was just too young. I didn't know how to tell you."

"I know that now." I took a deep breath. "You were too young and naïve and I was too old and set in my ways. I knew from the moment I met you that you were my forever love. But I didn't know if I was yours. I needed to know I was your forever love and not just your first love. So I decided to wait. I decided to let you grow up and do your own thing. If you loved me, really loved me, I knew you would come back to me."

"I've always loved you, Brandon." She looked at me with passionate eyes. "That's why I got a job at a company I knew you were buying."

"The day you applied to Marathon Corporation was the day that my life turned back to color. I was so excited. I knew that this was the moment I had been waiting for. But I knew that I had to be more careful this time. I couldn't just welcome you into my open and waiting arms. I had to test you, Katie. I didn't want to hurt you, but I couldn't let you back into our son's life without knowing that you weren't going to run again. I needed to know that you were strong enough to go through hell and still come back to me. This isn't a game, Katie. This is for real. This is for love. This is for our life. I needed to know that you were mature enough to deal with a family. A real family. You've already broken my heart once and it killed me. I can't have you breaking our son's heart as well."

"I would never do anything to break his heart." She whispered softly.

"If you come into our lives and leave again, it would break me and it would break him. He's already forming a bond with you." I took a deep breath. "I didn't mean to push you so hard. I didn't mean to hurt you, but I had to know that you would stay, no matter how much I pushed you."

"Oh, Brandon. I'm not going anywhere." She leaned toward me and kissed me. "Please don't test me anymore. I'm sorry I lied about being eighteen."

"Katie, I want you to remember one thing." I took her hand and held it to my heart. "It wasn't that you lied about being eighteen. I can live with a lie. You were young and it happens. It was that you had so many opportunities to tell me the truth and you didn't. Even to that last day, you told me you were going to a business lunch. I knew there was no business, Katie. I just wanted you to tell me the truth. I wanted you to prove to me that, despite your age, you were an adult."

"You knew?" Her eyes widened and I nodded slowly.

"I always knew," I whispered in her ear. "Remember when I talked about being eighteen and first loves? Remember when I told you I was going to be a guest lecturer? Remember when I told you we could get through everything if we were just honest with each other? I gave you so many opportunities to tell me

72

the truth. I so badly wanted you to tell me so that we could live our lives. But it wasn't to be at that time. You had to grow up."

"I can't believe you knew." She shook her head and I pressed my lips against hers softly. Her fingers ran through my hair and she kissed me back passionately. We fell back onto the bed, our hands exploring each other hungrily. I ran my hands down her back and under her top so that I could feel her skin. My fingers burned as they touched her and I felt a heat rising through me as she bit down on my shoulder.

"Wait just a second." I jumped off of the bed, ignoring the groans of my body as I walked to my closet and pulled out a small box. I walked back to the bed slowly, and Katie stared up at me with wide eyes.

"Katie." I got down on my knees and pulled her up so that she was sitting up and not lying down.

"Oh my God." Her hand flew to her mouth and I smiled.

"This isn't exactly how I had this planned," I laughed gently. "I thought we would be on a picnic somewhere and Harry would bring me the ring and stand behind me. I never wanted to do this in the bedroom or in the throes of passion. But I can't hold back. I don't want to hold back. I've never felt that a moment has been as right as this one is right now."

"Brandon." Her eyes glittered with unshed tears and I shook my head and smiled.

"I'm doing the talking now." I grinned as she rolled her eyes at me. "I knew I loved you from the first moment I saw you outside of Doug's, a place, by the way, we will never let our underage daughters go."

"We would never have met if I hadn't gone." She grinned at me and I gave her a quick kiss before pulling back.

"The day you came into my life with your gorgeous smile and your trusting eyes was the best day of my life. And our relationship was perfect. You were perfect for me. I was perfect for you. We were perfect for each other. I knew that in my heart. I always knew that. But I didn't want to capture a caterpillar in a jar and keep a butterfly hostage. I needed you to metamorph and come back to me. I needed to know that the beautiful butterfly had seen the world and knew that I was the one. And you came back to me, my sweet Katie. You came back to me, and all I want to do is hold you tight and never let go. I can't lose you again. I told you once that we were forever, that you were mine. I didn't mean that I owned you, Katie. I meant that you owned my heart. You were mine and I was forever yours. I love you. I've always loved you. Being without you for seven years has aged me more that you'll ever know. Marry me, my darling. Marry me and make me the happiest man in the world." I opened the box and slowly took out the ring I had bought for her all those years ago. "Will you marry me, Katie?"

"Yes, oh yes. Oh, Brandon," she gasped as I slowly slid the ring onto her finger, love emanating from my every pore. I pulled her into my arms and kissed her all over, feeling like I had finally won. Everything had finally come together and I was finally going to live the rest of my life with the woman I loved with all my heart.

***

I watched Katie and Harry playing with his new train set and felt content and happy. This is what I had been waiting for these seven years. I walked back to my office with purpose. It was time now. I could get rid of all of the documents Will and Matt had given to me.

I grabbed the key from my pocket and opened the safe, pulling out the files that were sitting there. I sat back and stared at the first file Will had given me seven and a half years ago, when I had first met Katie. I listened to Katie's laughter and smiled as I shredded the documents.

"Daddy, Daddy! Come and play with me and Mommy." Harry ran into the office with a huge smile on his face and happiness in his eyes.

"Just a minute, son."

"Okay." He rolled his eyes at me and I laughed. He looked just like his mother when he did that.

I stood up and looked at the final document in the folder, feeling a sudden release of pent-up emotion. This was the first piece of information I'd ever gotten on Katie, from a couple of days after we met. It was the information that could have and should have ended everything. I stared at the machine as it gobbled up her birth certificate and walked calmly back into the living room to spend time with the two people I loved the most.

"Who wants to play a board game?" I asked casually, sliding my arm around Katie's waist as she relaxed into me.

"Me, Daddy! Me!" Harry jumped up and ran to his room to get his games.

I laughed before whispering in Katie's ear, "Don't worry, my love. Tonight we can play our own games."

Katie's hand slid to the front of my pants and she grinned wickedly at me. "Who says we have to wait for tonight?"

Made in the USA
Lexington, KY
07 October 2014